In *The Upstairs*  ...ng
in terror from the ...
Now the war i... he
knew have changed forever.

"The book offers an intensely provocative story,
recalling many personal crises and tests of human nature
cruelly beset by the dangers and deprivations of war."
—*The Horn Book*

In honor of

THE JOURNEY BACK

THE JOURNEY BACK

Johanna Reiss

HarperTrophy®
A Division of HarperCollins*Publishers*

THE JOURNEY BACK
Copyright © 1976 by Johanna Reiss
All rights reserved. No part of this book may be used or
reproduced in any manner whatsoever without written permission
except in the case of brief quotations embodied in critical
articles and reviews. Printed in the United States of America.
For information address HarperCollins Children's Books, a division of
HarperCollins Publishers, 10 East 53rd Street, New York, NY 10022.

Library of Congress Cataloging-in-Publication Data
Reiss, Johanna. The journey back.
  Continues the author's The upstairs room.
  Summary: After spending three years hiding from the Nazis,
a Jewish family is reunited and begins the job of rebuilding
their country and family.
  1. Reiss, Johanna. 2. Jews in the Netherlands—Social conditions—
Juv. lit. 3. Netherlands—Social conditions—Juv. lit.
[1. Netherlands—History—1945-   2. Jews in the Netherlands]
I. Title.
DS135.N6R444   949.2'07'0924   76-12615
ISBN 0-690-01252-7.—ISBN 0-06-021457-0 (lib. bdg.)
ISBN 0-06-447042-3 (pbk.)

Published in hardcover by HarperCollins Publishers.

First HarperTrophy edition, 1987

To my daughters,
Julie and Kathy,
who were my guides

Foreword

It was the spring of 1945. The Second World War in Europe was over. Just as in the other countries the Germans had occupied, the people of Holland had been robbed of so much—loved ones, dignity, joy in being alive, and almost all their material things.

But they were free now, as were my sister Sini and I. We were Jews, and might have been killed if the Oosterveld family had not taken us into their house and hidden us.

While this book is a sequel to *The Upstairs Room*, it is complete in itself. Obviously I cannot assume that you have read the first book. Yet some knowledge of what took place in it is important. So, in this book I have written a little about the war years, to give you at least a feeling for what they were like.

The Journey Back is about what happened after the war ended, when the members of a family—mine—return home and are reunited, after almost three years of having been away and apart, in different places in Holland—and no longer know one another.

Part One

USSELO

It is not easy to find Usselo. On many maps of Holland you cannot find it at all, only on those that list every village, no matter how tiny. Not many people, however, care to know where Usselo is. Why, there is hardly anything there—fields, a café, a bakery, a school, a church and parsonage, a kind of dry-goods store in a house, and farmhouses, but only a handful of those. There's no more than that in Usselo. Such a quiet little village, where life was orderly and pleasant for years and years and years.

Sometimes there would be a wedding, or a funeral to which every farmer went, walking two by two behind the hearse, talking in hushed and not so hushed voices.

"Quiet, he's not buried yet." "But what's true's true. He was as dumb as a pig's ass. Take how he planted potatoes . . . no good . . . right smack next to each other . . . told'm so, too . . . wouldn't listen. He could never have gotten as many basketfuls as he said he did. If you ask me, I'd say he was a liar."

There were dances, too, in the café, where an accordion player pulled and pushed and pressed down on keys and buttons with fingers that were stiff from farmwork, while around him, legs waltzed and polkaed inside tight black pants and long black skirts, and lace caps slid off, showing hair that was stiff and shiny from sweet milk that had been rubbed on to make it so.

Year after year, every season, the same things happened in Usselo. In the winter pigs were slaughtered, and the farmers visited each other, sipping from glasses as they commented on the animal that was hanging from a ladder in front of them, cut open.

"She's got a tasty border of fat on'r, not like Willem's pig we just saw. . . ." "Some sausage this one will make— No, thanks, not another drop. Don't forget, we've got three more calls to make today. All right, a little bit then, to wet the throat."

And back on their bikes they'd go because soon it would be time to milk the cows.

During the rest of the year they saw each other, too, the farmers of Usselo. Outside, in the fields, behind plows and wielding sickles, on hay wagons, and as they were binding the sheaves of rye, wearing straw hats this time, against the sun; the women in white aprons with long sleeves but no gloves, their hands scratched and their nails broken. And they saw each other with baskets of seed potatoes on their arms, and turnips, and cabbage. They knew each other well. But then there were so few of them, not more than a handful.

The Oostervelds lived in Usselo, and had for over fifty years. Their farm was small. When Johan Oosterveld was a child, he went to the one-room schoolhouse, just like the few other children in Usselo. Sometimes he played soccer, as they did, but only sometimes and never for more than a short time. His father was sick; Johan was an only child, and even though the farm was small, there was a lot of work that had to be done.

"Johan, Joha-a-a-an, come home." And his mother would give him a piece of bread on which she had sprinkled salt, so he'd be able to taste the thin layer of butter better; before she sent him to get the horse and plow. And off he would go, down the road, to where the fields were. "C'mon, horse; come, come, come." It was not easy to make straight furrows in the soil. He was only eleven, Johan, and the plow was heavy.

His father continued to be sick for six more years. Johan no longer went to school at all, or played. He had no time.

"Too bad," his teacher said when Johan didn't come back. "That boy has brains, Vrouw Oosterveld. He could go far, become a teacher, like me. . . ." Instead it was "C'mon, horse; come, come,

come" year after year after year. But I did not know any of this then. How could I? I was not even born yet.

When Johan was seventeen, his father died.

"Take it easy for a few days now," his mother said. "Look around and find someone to marry. But, please, don't choose a girl from the city. They don't know what work is. Get someone with a good pair of hands, Johan, to help."

"Leave it to me, Ma," Johan said. "I'll see what I can do."

He looked around Usselo. Then in the next village, the one that was only half a mile away, he found Dientje. "Wait till you see her, Ma," he said. "She's got a real pair of hands on her—you won't believe how big they are. We can both take it easy from now on. She's a lot older than me, too. She must really know how to work. And I'll tell you something else. We're going to be rich. She's got a real—what-d'you-call-it—dowry. Some bedding, and this you'll love, Ma, five chickens and none of them scrawny. Maybe even a cow if I play my cards right. Eh?"

"My Johan," his mother said proudly, wiping her eyes.

After the wedding the three of them lived in the little farmhouse—Johan, Dientje, and Johan's mother—Opoe, as everyone called her, although she never did become a grandmother. And life went on. Orderly and pleasant enough, until— But not yet. There were more weddings and funerals to go to first, more plowing to do and harvesting and sausage making.

Johan and his mother still worked very hard. "It's funny, Ma, with such hands who would've thought. . . . Dientje always wants to rest."

While Johan, Dientje, and Opoe lived in Usselo, I was living with my family in another town, a much bigger one, Winterswijk, forty kilometers away, where my father was a cattle dealer. He used to take me with him in his car when he went to call on customers.

"De Leeuw, good to see you again," they'd say. "That little black-and-white cow you sold us is doing well, is giving even more milk than you said she would, but the milk is watery and we feel we paid too much. Does Annie want a cookie?"

Sure. I'd take one. I did not even have to choose. They were always the same—yellow with sugar sprinkles. "Thank you," I'd say to the farmer's wife. I'd try not to stare at the container, which was always put back in the same place it had come from, a cabinet on the wall, behind glass. I'd wait for Father to be ready, so we could leave, drive to another farmer, to another cookie with sprinkles. I liked going with him.

I liked many things. Being home with my two sisters, Sini and Rachel, if they were nice to me. They were much older—adults almost. With Mother—only she was always sick. With Marie, our maid, who let me sit on her back as she cleaned the floors on all fours. And I liked being with other children, friends, with whom I climbed trees, ran, and laughed. Life went on for us, too, in Winterswijk, in the big house in which we lived.

· 2 ·

Then the Second World War broke out in Europe. Adolf Hitler, chancellor of Germany, wanted his country to be big and powerful and glorious again, as it had been many times in history. Many Germans agreed, and joined his Nazi party.

It was 1939 and autumn when Hitler's army invaded Poland. "Go," he said to his soldiers, "and don't stop."

In less than ten months they had occupied Denmark, Norway, Belgium, Luxembourg, France, and Holland. They even found Usselo. It was May

1940. The members of the royal House of Orange, which had been reigning over our country for hundreds of years, fled. The enemy stayed.

Our lives did not change much—not right away. Father still went out in his car; Mother was still sick; Rachel and Sini continued to work. I was in school now, in the second grade.

And in Usselo? They barely knew there was a war. Not until the farmers had trouble getting enough feed for their cattle, and the enemy demanded a cow from everyone. Hitler's soldiers were hungry, and there were many of them.

"Goddammit, I think we've got a war on our hands, Ma, Dientje," Johan said angrily. He was even surer when the enemy wanted still another cow; eggs now, too, and copper, which they turned into bullets. But apart from becoming even poorer and having begun to curse, Johan's life had not changed: "C'mon, horse; come, come, come," furrow after furrow.

The enemy hated many people: gypsies, Slavs, Communists, priests, and almost everyone who was not German or who dared to disagree. Above all, Hitler hated Jews, and in every country his soldiers occupied, he began to make life especially hard for them. He forbade them to work, travel, shop, go to school. He forbade them more, and more. Until—

yes, now—Jews were being dragged out of their houses and off the streets and pushed into freight cars that were locked and cramped and without air.

"Go," Hitler yelled to his soldiers. "Go, go. Don't waste time." The trains left on Tuesdays for Austria, Germany, and Poland, for camps that were hard to pronounce—Mauthausen, Bergen-Belsen, Dachau, Auschwitz. Where they were murdered, the Jews and the others who disagreed. But most of them were Jews.

The Oostervelds did not like to hear about this. "Goddammit, Dientje, Ma, what kind of people are those Germans?" But it all seemed far away. Johan had seen a Jew only once in his life. "That good-for-nothing cattle dealer Cohen from the city, who pinched our cow in the nose when I said he wasn't offering enough money for her. She almost died."

There was just as much work to be done in the fields and around the farm, but life was no longer the same, no longer orderly, or even a little bit pleasant.

There were no more weddings to go to. Those who did get married made nothing of it. There was not enough food to give a party. The enemy, you know. No more sausage making, either—no pigs. The enemy. . . . Only funerals were left, but even they were no longer the same. The farmers were afraid to say much. What if they complained about the war—it was hard not to—and someone over-heard? Like Willem, who thought the Germans were wonderful—he might turn them in. The soldiers would come and take them away....

Two by two, they walked behind the hearse, the handful of farmers, with their mouths shut.

But their lives had not changed as much as ours. So much shouting at home. We were Jews. We didn't want to end up on those trains that left on Tuesdays.

"We must hide," Father said, "if I can find Gentile people who'll take us in." After a while he did find places for us. Secretly we left town, Father for a city near Rotterdam. "It will not be for long," he said. Half the world seemed to be fighting against Hitler now, and against Germany's partners, Italy and Japan. England was, France, Canada, Russia, the United States, other Allied countries. How long could the war last?

My sister Sini and I? We went to Ussello, to live with a family named Hannink. A few weeks later, Mother died and was hurriedly buried. Only then did Rachel leave, for a small village hours from Winterswijk. She was the last Jew from our town to do so. It was November, 1942.

· 3 ·

After a few months we could no longer stay with the Hanninks. It was too dangerous, Mr. Hannink said. The Germans were suspicious of him; they thought he might be hiding Jews. "If they find you here, we'll be murdered, too—my wife, my daughter, and myself. You must leave."

Late one evening, when it was dark out and no one could see us, Sini and I arrived at the Oostervelds' door. There they were, the three of them. Frightened, I looked at the man, Johan. He was big. His face was red, and he had brown hair that grew straight up. His cheeks were thin, hollow almost, as if for years the wind and rain had beaten on them and left dents.

"Hiya." He smiled around a cigarette butt that hung from the corners of his mouth. "Two Jewish girls. I'll be damned. Who would've thought it, Ma. Of all the farmers to choose from in Usselo, Mr. Hannink picked me. Ja, ja, girls, he's an important man. I bet he thought I was brave enough to take this big risk. Because that's what it is, a big risk. They could kill us all." He shifted the cigarette butt to the other side of his mouth.

"Let's see," he went on, "that little one, Annie,

must be about ten or eleven. The sister's a lot older, I'd say. Sure, Ma, look for yourself. About twenty, I'd guess." He walked over to his mother and took her by the shoulders. "Ma, after all these years you're really an Opoe. Eh? You like that?"

She did. She laughed up at him with her whole face, all her wrinkles, her toothless mouth. "Two girls at once, Johan. Nice ones, too."

Now I could laugh. It was all right. They liked us.

"*Ssht*," Dientje warned, "not so loud for God's sake." She looked scared. She reminded everybody of what Mr. Hannink had said. A few weeks, that was all. Then he'd take us back.

But Mr. Hannink never did. No one even mentioned it. Already we had been with the Oostervelds for months. Father had been wrong. Still the war. . . .

Sure, the Oostervelds were nice, very nice. But the days were long. So many hours in one day, so many days. On some, the sun was out; on others, not. Or it rained or not. We had to keep away from the window, so that no one could catch a glimpse of us and mention that the Oostervelds had strangers living upstairs. "I could swear to it. I looked up and there they were—two girls. Who can they be, I wonder? Eh?"

What if Willem heard? He'd tell the enemy. They'd come. "*Wo sind sie?*" they'd scream, and take us away.

Clop, clop. There was a farmer going by, his wooden shoes stamping outside. He had a horse with him, too. I could hear the hooves. Which way were they going? To the left? To the right? Down the road or up, and how far? To another town? Which one? Which one?

From where I was sitting, I looked at Sini. She had not said a word for hours. I looked at the wall, the ceiling, the floor, which was covered with speckled linoleum and took no time to cross—five seconds. Someday I'd get up; I'd walk out of this room and I'd keep on walking forever, through fields and meadows and across ditches. . . . When they were gone, the soldiers, and it was safe.

Finally the Germans were beginning to lose, in Russia and in Africa. Maybe they'd keep on losing now. I could hear myself running down the stairs already—*kla-bonk, kla-bonk*—on my way home to Winterswijk.

Maybe Father could take us somewhere, to celebrate. Would we go to the little hotel by the ocean where we used to spend our vacations? Without Mother though? I swallowed. No, a brand-new place would be better. I knew of one, too. Yes, yes.

Ssht, you almost made a noise. Can't. Quiet. Willem. . . .

It was an island called Walcheren in the south-western part of Holland, not far from Belgium. I had seen pictures of it in a big book, colored pictures, of hedges with red and white flowers that grew around fields and gardens. Hardly any of the people wore ordinary clothes. No, they wore old-fashioned ones—black pants, long skirts. They wore a lot of golden ornaments and beads, too. It would take a whole day to get to Walcheren, but I wouldn't mind. I'd sit close to Father, help him steer the car. "Careful, there's a tree." Oops.

Rachel would pack a picnic; there'd be pancakes with raisins for eyes. We'd stop by the side of the road—or, and this would even be nicer, we'd eat in the woods, hear birds, see tiny animals. But I wouldn't want to sit for long. I'd get up quickly to jump over the shafts of light that were coming through the trees. Here; no, there.

After a few minutes Father would want to leave. "C'mon," he'd say, and with his mouth still full, he'd hurry back to the car. "Rachel, Sini, Annie—last chance."

I smiled in the direction of the window. Father was a little impatient, but we hurried. We didn't want to get there after dark, either!

There were dikes all around the island of Wal-

cheren, high, high ones, to protect it from the
North Sea. I'd climb up on one, up and up, to the
top. And I'd stand sideways so that I could see
everything, land as well as water. Look how the
water sparkles in the sun! A boat sliding by as in
a dream . . . and a bird, a speck of white—

"Careful, don't fall!"

Silly Rachel. I wouldn't. It is very windy
though. My hair . . . I close my eyes to keep it out.
Now I can even hear the water as it crashes against
the bottom of the dike, far, far beneath me, swish-
ing and splashing, never stopping. . . .

"Look, it's raining again," Sini complained. "As
if it isn't already dark enough in the back of the
room."

At night it wasn't dark. The minute the Oostervelds were finished with their work, they'd rush
upstairs, pull the shades down, and turn on the
light.

"That's better, girls, right? Ja, ja, Dientje
knows." With a sigh she'd sit down, her hands
folded on her stomach. Once in a while she'd bend
forward and carefully touch my face. "I'm so glad
you're here, my little Annie," she'd say, and nod.

"Sini," Johan said, "I want you to tell me again
what Winterswijk looks like so I get a good picture
of it in my head." Carefully he'd listen. "Here, Ma

and Dientje are always saying things I've heard for years. 'Milk the cows, feed the horse, dig up the potatoes.' Bah, I know it all by heart. This, I like. It's giving me a new set of brains. Dientje, let's have some more of that coffee even though it's no good, and don't tell me that's because it's a substitute. I remember how it tasted before."

Dientje would wink at me.

"Watery, Johan," Opoe complained, "not the way I used to make it." She was peeling tomorrow's potatoes, a brown mountain of knobby shapes. *Plop, plop, plop*—one after another they fell into the pail, splashing a little, making Opoe's long apron wet. But she did not seem to care. *Plop.* "Look at this one, Annie." She held up a potato for me to see. "Can you tell how special it is? It's round, and it's got nothing sticking out?"

Enthusiastically I'd nod. "Yes, Opoe."

"It's going to be yours." She beamed. She rummaged through the peels, searching for another special one for Sini.

"I sure wish the other farmers could see me now," Johan said, "sitting here with my family."

I nestled deeper in his lap.

Time went on and on. Not fast, not at all. It was 1943 now, or perhaps even later. So many hours and minutes and seconds in each day. Rain or not . . .

getting colder . . . snow again. The sound of a sled. "Did you hear it, Sini?"

In the semidarkness I could see her head move. But which way?

The German army continued to lose, and little by little the Allied soldiers pushed them out of the countries they had occupied in the first few years of the war. The more they had to give up, the angrier Hitler became. "Take what you can from the countries you're in," he ordered his soldiers. "Clothing, machines, trains, food. Send home what you can't carry."

Many people were wandering through the countryside, begging farmers for a turnip, an egg, a cup of milk, anything. "Thank you, thank you," they'd say, and shuffle on . . . the way time did.

Uneasily the enemy watched the Allies approach Holland in the fall of 1944. But they had no intention of leaving, especially not the island of Walcheren in the southwestern part of Holland, that pretty island about which books had been written. From Walcheren the enemy controlled a port the Allies needed to bring in supplies.

When the Germans would not go, planes came, dropping pieces of paper that whirled from the sky, telling the sixty thousand islanders to leave. "There will be floods," the pamphlets said. "Go."

And many refugees from Walcheren, in their old-fashioned clothes, began to wander through Holland, too, begging for a place to stay. "Thank you, thank you."

A few days later, the Allied planes returned. When they reached the dikes, the high, high ones that went all around the island, their bomb bays opened.

The Germans left, but another enemy came in. Through four gigantic holes in the dikes, salt water from the North Sea rushed across meadows and fields, through hawthorn hedges, and over the red, purple, and yellow of fall gardens, into houses through cracks in doors and windows. Inside, the water climbed up over furniture, walls, and stairs, taking pictures from hooks, an empty cup that had been sitting on a table, a coal scuttle, a piece of bread, a blanket.

Those islanders who had ignored the Allies' warning and remained on Walcheren looked out from their attic windows in horror. They saw cats, dogs, and chickens floating by, their claws clutched around branches; a cow thrown on her back by a wave; petals, red and yellow and purple; vanes from a windmill; and some instruments that belonged to the brass band—a trombone, a clarinet.

Six hours later, when the tide turned, the water began to fall, just as it did on the other side of the dikes, and six hours after that, it began to rise again, on both sides. Now we would not be able to go to Walcheren for an even longer time. When anyway? When?

Again everything was so still outside. Another winter. No sounds again. Snowflakes make none when they fall; they only darken the room even more. Can't wait until tonight, until Johan, Opoe, Dientje— "Girls," they'd say, "we're here." And it would not be dark any longer.

· 4 ·

It was not dark now either. How could it be? The end of the war had come. Yes, now, in spring, 1945. It was all right to make noise again, to shout, jump, run, dance. Slowly I walked to the window. My legs hurt. I had been sitting down for so long, two years and seven months. But no more, no more. It was over. It had to be. This morning Willem was picked up and put in jail.

"Serves him right," the farmers yelled. "That numbskull, to have been a friend of the Germans.

We'll never talk to him again. You can be sure of that."

That's what people all over Holland were shouting as a hundred thousand more traitors shuffled through the streets, on their way to jail, too. Singing age-old Dutch songs, townspeople everywhere hung out the Dutch flag for the first time in five years. With every flutter, the red, white, and blue stripes with the orange-colored banner were shedding dust and cobwebs. "Look . . . ought to be ashamed . . . should have cleaned. . . ." "No time. . . . " Already they were in their gardens, planting marigold seeds so that soon there would be flowers again, orange ones, which the enemy had forbidden—orange, the color of the royal house. That much hate.

All over Holland there was music and dancing. On country roads rusty accordions were p-u---lled and p-u----shed into waltzes and polkas. In Amsterdam a barrel organ that had been hidden from the enemy was wheeled into the streets again, pouring ting-tingly music across the canals as the man turned the wheel. Faster, louder, while skinny bodies moved to and fro, not feeling hunger, not now.

There was no music in Walcheren. In the low-lying parts people waited for the tide to come in so that they could step out their windows and onto their rafts as they had for half a year now, steering with poles to keep to the right of the "road" while they floated to their errands or dates, their skirts and pants rolled up to keep them dry. Today, though, they wore paper flowers around their arms, orange ones. "Free. Free."

Near the dikes the people had time for nothing but work. Out of brushwood and reeds, mattresses were being woven that had to go down into the holes. Faster, faster. The winter storms were only seven months away. So little had yet been done. All four holes were still open. Yet, they were smiling, the men, that day. After all, wasn't Holland free! Couldn't people from other parts of the country come and help now! They paused, just for a second, to see whether a boat with workers was already in sight.

On the other side of Holland, in Usselo, I walked outside for the first time, tightly holding on to Johan's hand. Look how well I was doing already—halfway across the road now. For a second I took my eyes off my feet and looked up. Beautiful out, especially the sky. It went on forever. . . .

In the bunker in Berlin, Germany, where Hitler and his closest friends and helpers had gone to hide, there was nothing but gloom. Hitler was still certain that his soldiers would be powerful once more, any day now, and gain back every bit of land they had had to give up. He still hated Jews and all the others who had dared to disagree with him. He still thought they were the ones who were responsible for this war, not he, not his friends. On April 30, 1945, when he knew the war was lost, he killed himself, just before the Russians reached the bunker.

The war in Europe was over. It had taken the lives of twenty-five million people, from many countries, in many different ways, by bombs, on battlefields, in concentration camps.

In the woods in Usselo. Just this morning, when a farmer tried to dig up the copper pot he had not wanted to give to the enemy, he stepped on a land mine: twenty-five million and one.

"You've walked enough now, Annie." Gently Johan picked me up. "But already your legs are a lot better, what? There for a while you waddled like a little duck. I was worried."

It was a poor country the queen came back to. A great deal had been destroyed—almost the entire city of Rotterdam and much of many other cities and towns. Railroad bridges, telephone lines, factories, raw materials, warehouses—gone, or empty. Only the roads were full. People whose houses had been destroyed in last-minute combat joined all the others who were still wandering along the roads, looking for places to stay, for friends, relatives— and for food, always for food: "Please, please." Wandering on, looking.

Sini and I could go back to Winterswijk any time now. We didn't want to. We stayed another week. At night the kitchen was filled with farmers, listening to Johan as he practically shouted out what had gone on right in this house for the last few years.

They shook their heads in amazement. "How could that be? On this very road, and we never knew." "Johan, you should've trusted us enough to tell us. It wasn't nice, tricking us the way you did." "He was not afraid; he just said so. That's bravery for you. The danger that man put himself in."

"It was dangerous for Mother and me, too," Dientje told them.

"That Johan," they shouted, pounding him on the back. "We've got ourselves a hero in Usselo, fellows. A real one, our Johan Oosterveld."

The first time they said it he looked baffled. But he liked it; he was laughing now. "Who would've thought it? All my life I've done nothing but dumb work, and here they call me a hero."

They all laughed together, Johan the loudest.

We had to leave. That's what Rachel said when she arrived. Father said the same thing, a few days later, when he stopped in to thank the Oostervelds.

"Come, Sini, Annie, I want to take you home with me."

Home? Home was here. "One more week, Father." He, too, went back to Winterswijk without us.

"It's the craziest thing," Johan told the farmers that night. "Those girls don't want to go back," he said happily.

The day came, the hour, the minute.

"I'm sure going to miss them." Opoe was blinking her eyes. "I don't know what I'm going to do with myself now. The house is going to be so empty."

"I know, woman. I know." Johan's voice shook, too.

For the last time we walked around the house. In the good room, on the big chest along the wall, were the family portraits. One of Opoe in her Sunday apron—the black one with the dark gray flowers. Johan's and Dientje's wedding picture— Johan grinning, in striped pants and a special jacket; Dientje holding a tiny bouquet of lilies of the valley. And now that people knew we had been hidden there, a photograph of Sini and me.

"Our children," Johan said proudly. "Don't we look good there? The five of us?"

Sini and I nodded. Yes. We hugged again and again. Until the young man who was going to give us a ride became impatient: "Let's go."

Down the road we went. It was daylight now, not nighttime as it had been when we came, almost three years earlier. A tiny village, Usselo, just as Johan had said. Even tinier now. The bakery and parsonage had been destroyed by bombs, just before the end. We went past the school Johan had gone to. It was filled with Canadian soldiers, as many schools in Holland were. The store; the café; the fields, where an occasional plow was already waiting. That was all. I turned around to catch a last glimpse of everything before we rattled across a hole and went around the bend.

Maybe this afternoon I'd go with Father to call on one of his customers. "I've brought my youngest daughter along," he'd say, "just as I used to." I'd watch Father and the farmer clasp hands again. I bounced on the seat.

"One hundred and eighty guilders." "No, de Leeuw, I won't part with her for less than three hundred."

It could be—I sat up a little straighter—that

Bobbie, my dog, would come along. Maybe Father had already gone to get him and had brought him back. Was Bobbie standing by the house now, waiting, wagging his tail, ready to run over to me, bark, jump up?

Was that Winterswijk in the distance? Already? Nervously I licked my lips. It was such a big town, hundreds of times bigger than Usselo—at least. And it had so many people, thousands and thousands, and so many children, girls my own age—just thirteen. Stealthily I pulled my skirt down as far over my legs as I could. I moved a little closer to Sini until I was sitting right next to her. She put her arm around my shoulders. What would it be like?

Part Two

SUMMER

Suddenly the car stopped. No matter how hard the man tried, it would not start again. Desperately he put his foot on the gas pedal. Nothing happened. He pulled out the choke and moved his foot up and down again. Nothing. For a second he sat still. He seemed to be thinking. Then he turned around in his seat. "I was afraid of that," he said somberly. "The carburetor—it's finally died."

As he was looking up and down the road for an army truck to tow him home, Sini and I began to walk, tightly holding hands. It was mild, warm almost, yet it was only May. The early morning sun was trying to push its way through a cloud. For a second it did, shining on the road, on the broken tank lying on its side, a bird curiously looking in, and it lit up the white stone marker that said Winterswijk .6 kilometers.

Anxiously Sini looked at my legs. "Is it too far for you, do you think?"

Of course not. I smiled to show her she needn't worry.

A great many people were on the road. Most of

them were walking, carrying bundles the way we were. Others were resting, sitting on tree stumps, talking. A young woman was rubbing her feet; they were red, swollen.

"How are things where you came from?" one of the men called out to us. "That's where I'm going, north, over a hundred kilometers from here. I'll get there, too, even if it takes me a week. I want to see whether my old mother is still alive." Without waiting for an answer, he jumped to his feet and ran toward a delivery cart that was gradually coming out from a side road. "Hey, hey, stop," he yelled to the boy who was pedaling it. "Where are you going?" Laughing, the man got in. "This is my lucky day." The bicycle's wheels, which had no tires, made clicking sounds on the asphalt as the boy pushed on, north.

Close to me, Sini was talking about this afternoon. "I'm going to look up my friends, Annie; find out how they are, what they're doing. Maybe we'll all get together." She squeezed my hand. "I bet it won't be long before I'm back into things. None too soon, either. Come on, Annie."

Yes. I stretched my legs as far as I could. I was in a hurry, too. Let's see, where could I go? Not to Willy Bos's, of course. Her father must be in jail. Sure, he'd been a traitor, like Willem. But there was Frits Droppers. He even lived close by. I wouldn't be able to climb trees with him for a while, but there were other things we could do—sit in the grass, whittle sticks, have fun. Yes, yes, yes. After I got back from visiting a farmer with Father. Father came first.

And then there was Rachel. I shouldn't forget about her. She was such a good artist. Maybe she'd show me again how to draw and paint. She even knew how to make things out of wood! I was going to be so busy, I almost felt like holding my head.

We were very close to Winterswijk now. Just ahead, around the bend, would be the first row of houses, brick ones smack up against each other. They even shared a roof. But when we got there, the roof was gone. One long hole stretched out over the entire row. There were more holes, too, where the windowpanes used to be. A dog stepped out of one of those while his owner was locking the door.

We were lucky. Our house was still in one piece. Johan had seen it for himself when he had gone to Winterswijk, to make sure the roads were safe for us. The man with the dog was brushing a piece of charred wood. It looked like a table. With a broom made out of twigs, he swept off some of the black.

Behind him, on a clothesline, a pair of patched overalls billowed in the wind. It was Monday, laundry day, and a little breezy, just right for drying.

Rapidly Sini and I went on, past other people, past more rubble and holes, past the movie theater and the beauty parlor. All the fronts of the buildings were boarded up, just the way the furniture store, the shoe store, and most of the other stores around the marketplace were. "Opening again when merchandise arrives" was written on the boards. Only a grocery store seemed to be open. In front of it many people were standing in line, empty bags hanging on their arms. Their voices were excited.

"Aren't the Allies wonderful to have dropped food again?" "Six planefuls of it. They say there's plenty more on the way." "As soon as I heard, I ran over. I didn't even bother to comb my hair." "I just hope it gets here fast," a fourth woman added, tightening the sash around her skirt so that it wouldn't fall off. "Because if it doesn't, we won't be able to cook the food we bring home. It'll be time for the gas to be cut off."

"Of course, it's nice that the Allies drop food, but why part of it in the water? In the harbor of Rotterdam it fell, instead of on the soccer field where everyone was waiting. It'll be soaked. Why didn't they give the job to someone who knew what he was doing?"

"The police will get it for us," someone else said soothingly. "They've been swimming around for days, trying to rescue the stuff."

Suddenly Sini let go of my hand. "Gerrit, how are you?" And to me, "Wait here. You should take a rest anyway. I want to talk to my friends." She ran across the marketplace. "Gerrit, Gerrit, stop for a second! It's me!"

The people in the line turned their heads and stared at Sini. So did the man she called Gerrit. Sini was talking to him now. His mouth opened, stayed that way. "Don't you remember me?" Her voice was shrill. He shook his head. No.

I looked at the ground. Had we changed that much?

Bong, bong— What was that? I looked around.

Bong— Nervously I laughed. The church clock, of course. Bong— It struck nine more times. We were going to be late. Where was Sini? I looked, turned all around, looked again. Sini?

There she was, standing by a building with a group of soldiers. The notice penciled on a cardboard window read "English lessons here. Just opened." Some students came out.

"I is a girl," one of them said.

"No," her friend corrected her. "You am a girl."

They winked at the soldiers. "In soon days wait you here, we speak."

I put the bundle down. Silly, to have been so frightened. It had been nicer before though, on the road, when there were just the two of us.

I leaned against the wall of the church. I could hear Sini talking and laughing as if she had all day! I was going home by myself. I knew the way. I did not need her. "Sini."

She did not hear me. I took a few steps. Whispering, coming from the back of the line. Heads turned.

"Poor thing. Look at her. What this war hasn't done to us!"

"How can she even walk on them. So spindly."

"And crooked."

My legs wouldn't stay this way. I should tell them. I was going to go to a masseur, Sini said, do special exercises. They'd get straight again, just the way they used to be.

With my eyes fastened on Sini's back I waited. Near me were farmers with pails of flowers for sale. "Beautiful daffodils, jonquils. Look 'ere. . . ."

Sini started to turn around. I smiled, raised my hand a little. Come. She did. As I stuck out my hand and took a few more steps, I saw a notice on the café wall. "Nightly Dances," it read. "The Canadian soldiers cordially invite you."

Quickly now, through the Misterstraat, past streetlights without glass, past a store owner who was tearing down a shed, so he'd have boards to put across his empty window frames, too, and his neighbor who begged him for a plank, just one, for the window of his store.

One more street, the short one with the cobblestones. There, we were already on it, passing one little house after another. They were not damaged, not even the windows. Ahead of us was the railroad crossing, and there was the road—ours.

It was a straight road and long, with poplars on either side, poplars so tall that you had to bend your head way back to see the beginning of the leaves. Beyond the trees were ditches, then meadows and farms—small ones. Only one house wasn't a farmhouse—ours.

We couldn't see it, not yet. Soon, though, part of it would be visible—the chimney, painted white like the rest of the house. In the meadow to our left a cow was grazing around molehills that stuck up like tiny black dunes. There was a piglet, too, all pink, and some sheep. A woman was tugging at the barbed wire on which fluffs of wool had caught. She must have heard us. She raised her head. We stopped.

"Hello, Vrouw Droppers. How have you been?" we said, and went a little closer. Maybe I could ask her about Frits. We were about to cross the plank. We didn't. She was staring in such a funny way and shaking her fist at us.

"Why did you have to come back?" she yelled. "You should've been killed. It's all because of you. . . ."

What did she mean? Fast, away from her, whatever she had meant. Part of our house was in view now, the chimney and one whole side. I held tightly to Sini's hand as we hurried on.

"Girls!"

Was that her? Coming after us?

"You didn't even see me you're in such a hurry. It's me, Maria!"

Sheepishly we laughed. Sure, we remembered Maria, the woman who always had a goat with her.

"It's nice to see one Jewish child back," she said to me. "Ja, ja, it's been a bad time for a lot of people. Take your neighbors, the Droppers. They lost their oldest son. You remember 'm—Hans. He tried to save a Jew's life by pulling him off a train before it left for Poland. A stranger yet. The Germans saw what he was doing and shot him right at the station." She paused. "The Droppers may not be very friendly," she warned. "They hate all Jews now. Well—" Maria changed the subject. "You girls must wonder where's the goat. Ja, she's gone. I go faster without her.

"That reminds me, I have to hurry. I never handed in my radio as others did. It's old, like me, but we both work." She beamed. "I just heard we'll have no trouble getting food next winter. The first freight trains are already being hauled home and will be running again by Christmas, for sure." She started to leave. "People are counting on me. They even stop me in the street to ask, 'Maria, what's going on?' No newspapers. That's why, I guess." Briskly she walked toward town.

We were in front of the house, on the path that led to the back door.

"Father and Rachel will take care of you now, Annie."

What? Sini didn't want to any more? What did she mean? But there was no time to ask. The door opened, and out ran Father and Rachel. We hugged, we kissed, we cried. We were back again —at last.

· 2 ·

Still holding on to one another, we walked inside, talking, asking about things but not waiting for answers. "How are you?" "Fine." "And you?"

"Fine." And out of the kitchen. Sini and I had to see the rest of the house. "Come," we said, laughing shyly and pulling each other along.

There was very little furniture, though, and the floors were bare. I tried to tiptoe. Still, the living room looked beautiful. There, as if they had never been away, were the old sofa and the chest with the tea cozy perched on top, a little bit of the teapot showing. And in the middle of the room, where they always used to stand, were the chairs with the plush seats that scratched your legs.

"Annie, put on something longer," Mother used to say, "or don't sit on those chairs."

I had anyway, telling her it was fine, but secretly I had put my hands underneath my legs and wondered why Mother loved those chairs so. I was glad they were back, though.

I had not thought about Mother for a long time. I stood there for a minute; then I rushed up the stairs to catch up with the others.

My room was much bigger than the one at the Oostervelds, gigantic almost. I bounced on the bed —perfect. Then I went to the window. Sure, just as I'd thought. Through the treetops I could see the clock on the church tower.

In Rachel's room there was something new— wooden plaques with Biblical sayings painted on them. Funny, we never had those in our house before. She must have made them herself. They were pretty, with curlicues and flowers everywhere.

"Come, Annie."

Yes, yes. I stepped out on the balcony, too. The road stretched out ahead of us. There was the Droppers' farm. Then, a little farther away, Mulder's, Ten Riet's and Geerdes', where the vanes of the windmills were going around and around. I could even see Maria's cottage at the very end of the road, and behind it, the woods, a long dark shape. Not safe. Might be mines there. . . .

There. I smiled. Old Geerdes and his two sons —one tall and one short—were rushing off to work, their shovels across their shoulders, exactly as they always had. "They never stop working," Father used to say. "Maybe that's why they have no furniture in their house. It would only tempt them."

"Hurry up, boys," old Geerdes was shouting. "We don't want your mother to be the first one digging."

Back in the kitchen we kept offering each other chairs, but only I sat down. The others were too restless. They were talking, talking, talking—about the rubble on the other side of town, how lucky Father was to have a bicycle with real tires yet, how tall the weeds in the garden were when Rachel first came back.

"And the house"—Rachel's hands pointed everywhere—"filthy, Sini. Those traitors who lived here while we were gone must never have cleaned. The dirt on the floors and walls was an inch thick. There's no soap. You can't imagine how hard I worked." She showed Sini her nails. "And it doesn't even look as if I made a dent. Those Judases must have expected to go to jail, too. Everything was gone from the house—dishes, pots. Not even a spoon was left.

"I borrowed a handcart, visited everyone we had stored our furniture with. 'Please,' I said, 'we're back.' Those Droppers cried when they saw me, but not from happiness. They threw a few things out on the road, then slammed the door in my face. Some other people returned nothing. I wanted to go to the police, to complain, but Father would not let me."

"How could we prove it was ours?" he said. "I did not ask for a receipt."

He was afraid, Rachel said angrily; that was why. "Didn't want people in town to think badly of us."

"Don't forget, I have to begin my business all over again. I can't afford to start with trouble. 'Look at that Ies,' they'll say, 'barely back and a big mouth already.' What if they continue to do business with the people they used while I was gone?" Impatiently, Father walked to the door.

Would he take me with him? Yes, yes, I had been right.

"Let's go, Annie."

Quickly I followed him outside and climbed on the back of his bicycle.

Rachel rushed after us. "Button your sweater," she cautioned. "I don't want you to catch a cold."

A cold? In this weather? Okay, if it was that important to her. I let her button it. Now we could leave, right?

"Make sure you stop plenty of times to rest, Father. Yesterday you came home exhausted."

"Stop bothering about me, Rachel. I have to go." Father's voice sounded a little edgy.

Rachel stepped back. Father put his leg over the bar, and off we went. It was wonderful, even more so than I had thought it would be. We whizzed along the road, leaving the poplars, the cow, the sheep, and the piglet behind us. Vrouw Droppers was gone. It did not matter that Father had no car. I could sit much closer to him this way. Contentedly, I rubbed my face against the back of his jacket. Even the sky was beautiful, with only a few clouds now, streaky ones, lacy almost, going east and rushing along fast like us. Which farmer would we go to? I had not thought to ask. Maybe to one who lived hours away.

Oops, the cobblestone street. We were slowing down. *A-bump, a-bump*, we went.

"Hang on, Annie."

I could not hold Father more tightly than I was. We were really slowing down. Maybe I should get off for a few seconds. "Father?"

He had already stopped. Drops of sweat were running down his face. "I'll have to leave you here, Annie. You won't have too far to walk home. I can go faster alone. The cow may already have been sold if I take too long to get there. But I'll come home as soon as I've finished." He kissed me, then continued down the street. Not quickly though, and his back was still bent.

In a couple of weeks, it would be better. When he was stronger, he'd ask me to go with him again. Then we'd get there, all the way.

Slowly I started home, across the rusty railroad tracks and through the weeds that had grown up all around them, past the poplars, the same ones, with the skinny trunks. Look, though! I bent down and put my hand on the ground right next to a tree. Moss, like velvet almost it was that soft, was growing against the bark. I bent down even more and smelled it. Musty but fresh, too.

I heard a dog bark. I struggled to my feet. Bobbie? No. It might have been though. He had run away from the people who were taking care of

him, Father said. Sure, that was a few years ago.
Still. . . . Calling his name over and over again, I
walked toward the house.

It had been a strange afternoon. Rachel never
stopped bustling around; Sini sat, in a daze; I
yawned. The light that came into the kitchen
started to grow dim. It was falling now only on
what was close to the window. The table, set with
the four plates. Father. For the first time since our
return, I studied his face. It was thin, with many
more wrinkles or with deeper ones; I didn't know
which. Almost all his hair was gray.

Rachel looked different, too—pinched, pale, older. They were like strangers almost, both of them,
not like family. I was glad Sini was here. I did not
have to turn my head to know what she looked
like—pretty.

"Father, Sini, Annie, come to the table," Rachel
said.

We sat down. Such a good place I had, right
opposite the window. I could see almost a whole
meadow, and anyone going by. It was very silent
though. It had been for a few hours now, with only
Sini and me doing a little talking, in whispers. *Ssht*,
Father was going to say something.

He started a few times, got out "I'm a happy
man tonight," and that was all. We could begin to

eat, I guessed. I picked up my fork and stuck it in a potato. Confused, I stopped. What was the matter with Rachel? Her head was bent, her hands folded. *Ssht.*

"Bless this food, O Lord. . . ."

"Not again," Father muttered. "Enough."

Then, except for the clinking of our forks, it was silent. Maybe Father would say something else? Or Sini? Or Rachel? Or me? What though? Just anything? I stared at my plate. It had been nicer in the Oosterveld kitchen. Much, much. There had been laughter and noise.

"Get your butt off the chair and pour me another plateful of that pudding, woman," Johan would say. "Why d'you think I married you, eh? No, Ma, you sit. It's Dientje I'm talking to."

Was it only this morning that Sini and I had left them? How could that be? It didn't make sense that we didn't live there any longer. I forced another bite down, and another, till my plate was empty.

Instantly Father pushed his chair back. It scraped across the tiles, but not so loudly that I couldn't hear what Rachel was saying: ". . . not for our sake, but for the sake of Jesus. Amen."

She opened her eyes and leaned toward me. Before her hand could touch mine, I got up.

Plop. Suddenly the electricity went on. Rachel had expected it and had already turned the switch. What now? Would we play a game? We used to, on special nights. The one where we all got eight cards? Maybe, maybe.

Father was putting a hand in his pocket. Yes? Yes? There, he had pulled out a piece of paper. He pulled out a pencil stub. He licked the point. He began to write. But not our names, the names of cows. "Marietje, red and white, two years old." Prices—of cows, rows of them. Additions and subtractions—cow ones.

Rachel sat down on the chair opposite him. Her lips began to move, too. Once or twice Father scowled at the Bible in her lap. Rachel did not notice. Leaning against Sini's chair, I watched. Row after row. Page after page.

Startled, I looked up. The doorbell was ringing. At this hour? Who could it be? Father went to look.

"Evening, Ies." Country voices.

And Father's happy one, answering, "Come in, Ten Riet, Mulder, Geerdes, Geerdes, Geerdes."

"Ah, but just for a minute, Ies. We know this must be a celebration for you."

Ten Riet stepped forward. "Ies, Rachel, Sini, Annie, now that you're home again we want to welcome you officially back into the neighborhood. It's different from greeting you out on the road as some of us already have done. We're glad. Only not that Mrs. de Leeuw wasn't allowed to see this day, and that Droppers refused to come along—I asked'm—and that our womenfolk couldn't; they're busy with the work." He pulled a rumpled handkerchief from his overalls and wiped his face.

He must have forgotten something. Mulder was nudging him with his elbow. "Oh, ja. And we came because it wouldn't 've been right not to, now that we know you're back. They made me the neighborhood chairman, Ies," Ten Riet complained, starting on his face again. "I hate to talk, but what can I do? I was picked, and now I'm stuck."

"Only till January first, Ten Riet," Mulder reminded him. "Then we'll vote again." He snapped his suspenders.

"Look at him! He thinks he's already got it," the short Geerdes son said, laughing.

Rachel went into the living room and came back with chairs.

"Not for the boys and me, Rachel," the Geerdes father declined. "Once we sit, we won't work." He took his pipe out of his mouth and peered into the bowl. "I can't wait till there's tobacco again," he grumbled. "I'm tired of sucking air."

"Only another month," Mulder comforted him, "and you'll be all right again. An ounce a week, Maria heard."

They weren't leaving, were they? Anxiously I watched Mulder give Ten Riet a signal. Good, Ten Riet had not noticed. He was too busy listening to Father talk about cows. "Ja, ja. Ja, ja, ja, Ies. . . ."

Mulder gave the signal again, a bigger sweep with his head.

I smiled. Again it had not worked. Of course not. Father knew so much about cows. "Ja . . . ja, ja . . . ja. . . ."

"Ten Riet," Mulder warned, "don't bother Ies with your stories tonight."

Hastily Ten Riet got up. "Ies, Rachel, Sini, Annie, we've got to go, which is only right. It's your first day back. But we can tell our wives and mothers that you all look well. We saw."

Led by Mulder, they hurried toward the door. The last ones to leave were the Geerdes sons. They could not take their eyes off the empty chairs. Then they were gone, too.

"In half an hour the lights must be off," Father ordered. Then I heard the door to his room close. I looked out my window. The lit dial on the church clock said nine. I took off my clothes and put them on the chair. Actually the room in Usselo had been a little cozier than this one, now that I was taking a better look at it. I quickly crawled into bed. Footsteps coming up the stairs. I smiled. They were Sini's. She must have forgotten what she said this morning, about not wanting to take care of me any more. Quickly I made room on the bed for her to sit by me.

"I miss Johan and Dientje," she began the minute she came in. She closed the door. "I don't like being here. It's not what I dreamed it would be. I had hoped Rachel and I would get on as we did before, but all she's interested in is work and her new religion. And Father isn't any better. I know it isn't easy for him, but the few times he stopped to say something to me tonight, he ordered me around as if I were a child—'Do.' 'Don't.' Doesn't he know I'm twenty-three years old? And my friends. . . ." She bent her head. "I don't want to see them, Annie, not after what happened with Gerrit. He must have thought I wouldn't make it back, the way he looked at me. I have to do something. I want to have fun, and have it fast. I've lost so much time already! I can't sit around here waiting!"

Awkwardly I patted her. Father and Rachel would not always be this busy. This was only the first evening. It was going to get better, maybe even as soon as tomorrow. And then we could do

things, all of us. Besides, she should not forget that
she had me, which was as good as having a friend.
Better.

We sat close, talking about the Oostervelds,
laughing a little again. The church clock struck
once. Half an hour had gone by. Sini got up, kissed
me. "Good night, my Annie," she said. Immediately afterward she ran out of the room.

A few minutes later I heard her at the front
door. Downstairs, from Father's room came "Sini,
is that you?"

She answered.

"Now? At this hour? You should be in bed.
What's the matter with you?" His voice had
become louder and louder.

The door closed behind her. "Sini, for an hour
then. No more. You hear me? Sini?" I heard him
run to the kitchen. "Rachel. . . ."

The fuss he was making. What was wrong with
going out? Nothing. When people were free they
could do anything they wanted to. Right? I could
not hear any more, not till the yelling began again.

"From the moment I set foot in this house, that
Bible has annoyed me. But I figured it would be
over once we were all back. I guess I was wrong.
A daughter of mine acting like a Christian, reading
the Bible, praying at the table. It's a good thing

your mother can't see it. But I don't want to see it, either. I've had enough. You're no longer with the people who hid you. You're—you're home. Put it away, I said."

Then Rachel's voice saying no, she wouldn't. A door slammed, Father's. He had gone back to bed.

My head felt dizzy. So much had happened today. The trip from Usselo. The long walk. Meeting Vrouw Droppers. Being home. Saying good-bye to the Oostervelds. The farmers' visit. That had been nice.

What were the Oostervelds doing now? Were they in bed, too? I got up for a second to see what time it was. Yes, ten minutes ago they would have gone upstairs. I could imagine Opoe sitting against her four pillows, her nightcap on, the strings tied under her chin. "Fui-fui," she'd be saying. "How can this be? Another night. I've already had seventy-three years of 'em, every one sleepless. Bah!"

"Good night, Opoe," I whispered. But she would not be able to hear. She'd be asleep already.

In the room next to Opoe's, in the brown four-poster bed, were Johan and Dientje. Near them, on a hook in the wall, hung their clothes—Johan's overalls and Dientje's dress with the stripes everywhere but on the sleeves and collar. "That would've been a pity, Annie; it's only for work." They were talking, about tomorrow.

"You've got to clean the stable, Johan, now that the cows are out in the meadow. And Johan. . . ."

"What?" Muffled, with his fist against his cheeks.

"The cows' tails have to be washed. Should've been done before this. I don't want anyone pointing at 'em and saying they're dirty. The plowing, too, Johan, for the cabbages and the potatoes. 'S got to be done. Piet already began yesterday, I saw. And Johan. . . ."

He was pulling the down comforter over his ears, and no matter how many times Dientje nudged him, he no longer answered. Then she lifted her hand over her head and pulled the cord. Dark. I knew. I had seen her do it so often. On about a thousand nights.

Dark here, too, and cold, even under the blanket. I shivered. I hated this room, the chair, the big window with the view of the church clock, the table with the little cloth. Did Sini have to go out? Couldn't she have waited a few more days? Even one?

I turned over. Then I turned over again. And again. I could not go to sleep. I buried my head in the pillow and stuck a finger in each ear. Still I could hear it—the dance music. From far, far away, from the café at the marketplace. Where Sini was.

· 3 ·

A few days went by. Every morning, around six, Father left, so he'd catch the farmers while they were still milking their cows. And every morning, just before he got on his bicycle, Rachel would open her window and remind him to be back in time for dinner.

If he answered, his voice was sharp. "I'll come back when I can, Rachel."

Shortly afterward Rachel would begin to clean. I could tell. The bucket she carried around made noises whenever she put it down. *Klt, klt.*

She should not work as hard as she did, Sini said when she and I came down for breakfast. "What difference does it make if it takes a week longer to get the house clean? That's not important, Rachel. Why don't you sit down for a while—do nothing? Let's talk, the way we used to. Remember the boy-friend you had? The sweet one who came in all the way by train to see you?"

But Rachel was not interested. She no longer had time to spend on such meaningless things, she said.

Sini and I began to scrape, rinse, and dry the floor, too, looking out the window to see what the weather was like. It wasn't too bad. Sini dried her hands and put her rag away. "I've had it for today,

Rachel, but be sure to leave my part. I'll finish it tomorrow. Let's go, Annie."

I, too, ran out of the kitchen. As I closed the door, I heard Rachel say, "Fortunately there's someone in this house who doesn't mind a little hard work." But she didn't sound as if she meant it.

The following day it looked as if Rachel were finally going to take a break. The door opened. She walked out without the pail or the rag, across the gravel path along the side of the house, to the strip of grass where Sini and I were lying. But she had not come to get a tan. She had come to tell Sini something, and it had to do with the cleaning. "If you can't be bothered with that, Sini, the least you can do is the shopping. There aren't enough hours in the day for me to stand in line, too."

"Of course not," Sini apologized. "I'm sorry." She got up immediately.

"You don't have to go, Annie," Rachel called after me. "My goodness, Sini can do that much herself. Why don't you stay home and rest?"

I shook my head. No. We left.

"To tell you the truth, Annie, I'm glad to get away from this house," Sini said.

So was I. Tightly holding her arm, I walked to town with her.

There was a great deal of activity in the streets

of Holland. Gangs of children roamed through them, looking on sidewalks and in gutters. If they were lucky and found a cigarette butt, they peeled off the paper, brushed off the burned end, and put the tobacco in a tin, which they would sell when they had filled it up. Sometimes they were extra lucky and found other things the Allied soldiers had thrown away—a piece of chewing gum still in its wrapper, half a cookie. When they found nothing on the sidewalks or in the gutters, they looked in other places—the backs of army trucks, for example—and took.

The streets were crowded with traitors, too. They wore jail pants, as they cleared away the rubble. "Don't you dare take a break, you hear! Keep on working," the guards shouted. "We want to get rid of this mess, and fast. Come, put more on those shovels. This is nothing compared to what you did to us."

Almost every town had a Maria, too, who hurried through the streets with the latest news. "Suits for men are coming, all the way from America. And pieces of chocolate, as soon as there's enough coal to get the machines going. No, no, the announcer did not say what sizes. Also, the fishermen threaten to strike, so don't count on the herring I mentioned yesterday. Their wives are demanding soap for the smell, and they want more tobacco."

And the news rushed on, to other streets and other towns, where other people stood in line.

In Winterswijk, a lot more stores had opened: the butcher's, the dairyman's, the baker's. But when, at last, the people came out, their bags were only a little fuller than they were when they went in, even if they had used up all their coupons. And on they hurried, to the next store, the next line.

"Have they run out of milk already?" a woman with huge eyes asked Sini. "No? There's still hope, you said?" Contentedly she sighed. "Things are getting better all the time, aren't they? Take a month ago—we had nothing. All I had to make stew with were potatoes. Now I can put in carrots, and if I slice them thin, it even looks like a lot."

Another woman, wearing the old-fashioned clothes of the people of Walcheren, agreed. "And if I can get to the butcher before he runs out, I come home with an ounce of meat, too."

The first woman smacked her lips. "I bet my husband won't even want to go to work. He'll want to stick around and eat by three in the afternoon."

"I hope they're feeding my husband well," said the refugee from Walcheren. "The back-breaking work he has to do to mend the dikes. Heavy, heavy rocks he handles all day long. To think it's only the first hole they're filling in. At this rate, I'll never get back. It's a mess there. People throw their garbage out the windows. They figure it'll wash out to sea anyway." She shook her head in anger. "They shouldn't do that. It brings in rats. God knows what I'll find when I do get home. A garden that's ruined for years to come, that's for sure. Right now I would've had such beautiful tulips and irises." Enviously she looked across the street, to where the farmers were selling their flowers. "If I can at least get back in time to plant something for next year— but what'll grow in that salty soil?"

"Ja, ja. I know what you mean," someone sympathized. We all moved up the line.

Nervously the woman with the huge eyes counted the number of people ahead of her. "Twenty-six. C'mon, c'mon! There's the egg I want to get and the onion I have to buy. It takes the whole day."

"It sure does," Sini answered. She sounded impatient, too.

Was she tired of shopping already? Unhappily I looked up at her. She must be. She was looking over toward the café, the same café from which the music would come in a few hours. "Gonna Take a Sentimental Journey," they would play. And she'd go. Dance. Miserable tune.

· 4 ·

The first night Sini was not home by ten, Rachel became more and more worried. "Maybe she has been in an accident, Father. With no streetlights working, it's pitch-dark out."

"Ah, she's all right." He shrugged his shoulders, but when he picked up his pencil again, he looked a little worried, too. Twenty minutes went by. Every time we heard a sound outside we looked up. But it was never Sini. It was the bleating of sheep, the wind blowing, the clop-clopping of a farmer's wooden shoes.

"Father." Rachel's voice was urgent. "I want you to go to town and look for her."

The only response was an angry grunt.

"Father, if you don't go, I will," Rachel threatened.

My goodness, Rachel was making a fuss. Sini was perfectly capable of taking care of herself.

"Father—"

"Damn that Sini." His chair fell over as he got up. "Dancing, dancing—that's all she has on her mind. Not another thought, I swear. Dancing. As if that's all there is to do in this world." On his way out, he noticed me. "Don't look so scared, Annie. Come, go to bed. I'm sure she's all right. Nothing happens to that one. She's just—" He left, closing the door with a bang.

I hurried upstairs to look out the window. It was too dark to see anything. What if Rachel had been right and something had happend to Sini? I stayed where I was, listening.

There, that was Sini's voice. "I have never been so humiliated in my life, making a fool out of me. If you ever come after me again, I don't know what I'm going to do, Father, but I won't go with you—that, I can tell you."

Smiling, I went to bed. She was home.

The next night Sini stayed out even later. Rachel looked furious, but Father was not there to complain to or to send to town. Too many cows had to be bought and prices haggled over. There weren't enough hours in the daytime to do it all. "From now on, Rachel, I will have to work at night as well." And he left, right after he said it, before he could hear what Rachel was shouting—that he had always left her with the responsibility for everything.

I didn't like being at home with Rachel and her Bible, either. Would she go on like this forever? That's what Sini said could happen. "And Rachel will have gotten nothing out of life."

If school would only begin, I'd have work to do.

Plenty of it. And there'd be real books—French, English, all kinds. I drummed my fingers on the table.

"Do you want me to read to you, Annie?" Rachel put her hand on the empty chair next to her. "Come, sit with me." I didn't want to. At the door I turned to look at her. Her head was bent again, over another page written by that apostle Matthew, whom everyone but Jesus had despised. I walked up the stairs.

I wished I could write to Johan and Dientje. Nights were long here, with no one really to talk to. But there was no mail delivery yet—not to Usselo anyway. I could think about them though, as much as I wanted. All I had to do was sit still, pretend; and I was there, with Opoe, Johan, and Dientje.

· 5 ·

We were not the only Winterswijk Jews who had come out of hiding. A few others had, too. Every day they met in the middle of the marketplace. By the tree, the same tree the enemy had marched up to during the war, carrying hammers and sharp nails, to put up notices that said Jews could no longer shop, go to restaurants, movies, parks . . . or

do much of anything except get on those trains—
the ones that left on Tuesdays.

Again the tree spoke, only in hushed tones now,
when a man from Town Hall put up a list of names
of all the Dutch Jews who had survived the Nazi
concentration camps. Trembling, the people at the
marketplace searched for names that were familiar:
"Jakob Vos . . . don't see . . ." "Please, Emma
Cohen. . . . no." "Mozes Spier. . . . His name isn't
here."

After they had looked at the list again and again,
they slowly started to leave, comforting each other,
saying that maybe the next time those names would
appear.

One of the women saw me and stopped. "You
are Ies de Leeuw's youngest daughter," she said.

I nodded. Pretty hair she had, brown and wavy.
Who is she? I wondered. She was staring at my
legs.

"My God, they're worse than they told me. You
look like a midget."

For a second I looked at her. I blinked. No, no
crying. Not now. Silently I left. It was almost four
o'clock, time to go to the masseur. Again.

I walked slowly. What if the exercises weren't
helping? Did other people think that, too? That I
was a midget? I swallowed.

But I was doing all right. I must be. The masseur said I was.

Although the man from Town Hall came only once a week, the Jews came every day. Just to make sure they had not missed a name yesterday. At last the tree mentioned the name of someone from Winterswijk—a woman, Mrs. Menko. Anxiously the people pushed each other away from the new list, to see for themselves. "Yes, yes, there is her name. 'Liberated in Bergen-Belsen. Menko, Hilde, 1904. Winterswijk.' Hilde Menko. Look, look! No, no, she's the only Menko I see. Not the rest of the family."

"Excuse me." The woman with the wavy brown hair tried to get closer. "If Hilde lived through it, maybe my husband did, too. They were both in the same camp. Let me see . . . Jakob Vos. Let me see. . . ." Rapidly her finger moved down the list. When she came to the end, she was wiping her eyes.

Mrs. Menko returned to Winterswijk in an army car, lying on her other nightshirt. It was late afternoon and getting dark, and they had been on the road for a long time.

"Where shall I take you, Mrs. Menko?" the driver asked her.

"Home," she whispered, "please." She raised herself a little, to help him look.

Slowly he drove through the streets. "Tell me where I should stop."

"Not here . . . no . . . no. . . ."

For the second time he wove through town. "You must find it quickly," he warned. "Soon it will be really dark, and you certainly won't be able to recognize your house."

She looked and looked. "So confused," she sobbed.

"Don't worry," he said, "we'll find it. Winterswijk is not that big. But I wish you remembered your address!"

At last he stopped at the police station. Two policemen came out, carrying flashlights. For a second they looked at her. She was covered with boils—even her scalp. Trembling, they carried her inside. She was light, although she was tall. Fifty pounds only.

After they had checked the register and found out where she had lived for twenty-five years, they said she could not go there. "Not yet, Mrs. Menko. Who would look after you? When you're stronger." They took her to the hospital instead.

"I don't see how she can pull through," Father said softly. He had just been and seen.

· 6 ·

What a beautiful summer, people said, hardly any rain. Which was lucky, they added right away, since there were so many who were still living outdoors or in houses that had no roofs. In the orchards the trees were heavy with fruit—apples big enough to be almost a meal in themselves. In the fields and gardens, the cabbage plants were shooting up as if they were being pushed. "It's going to be some harvest," people said, laughing already, just thinking about it.

On Sundays the churches were filled, with many people giving thanks for many things.

Rachel was there, too. She left the house very early, before anyone else was up, closing the door softly behind her. A few hours later she would come back, her face bright and happy. In the afternoon the church bells rang again and once more Rachel rushed off.

With his hands jammed in his pockets, Father watched her go. He wished the soldiers had stolen the church bells, and turned them into bullets. They had in many other towns. The sound of them was driving him crazy. And on Sundays he began to go out, too—for his business.

I had often passed them before, the group of children. I even knew in which houses along the cobblestone street most of them lived, and exactly where they played, throwing balls, running, giggling, shrieking, or just standing around. But they had never before stopped what they were doing when they saw me or looked at me in this way, as if they were waiting for me.

They were coming over. All of them? Yes, all six. What did they want? Were they going to chase me, shout Jew in my ears again, hit and kick as kids had done years before?

I walked faster. They did, too. Their voices. That close already? I still had a good distance to go before I'd be home—more than half.

They were right next to me now. In a second, they'd begin. Please, no.

"Were you really hidden as people say?" one of them began.

I stopped. "Yes." Nervously I licked my lips.

"Did the Germans ever catch you?" "You escaped?" "Any shooting?" "They hit you?" Curiously they pressed closer. "What was it like?" "What did you do?"

"Nothing," I whispered.

Unbelieving, they looked at me. "Nothing? For all that time?"

"The Germans had their local headquarters in the downstairs of the house I stayed in." My voice sounded a lot louder now. "It was scary."

"Did they catch you then?" one of the boys demanded.

"Well—no," I confessed. "But don't think it wasn't dangerous. I had to stay in bed all the time, so they wouldn't hear me, and once —"

"What?"

"A soldier saw me," I said triumphantly. But, no, nothing had happened then, either. Ashamed, I dropped my eyes.

"Let's go back," I heard one say. When I looked up, they were already doing that.

But wait. One of the girls had turned around, the older one. "What school will you be going to?" she asked.

"The M.U.L.O.," I said proudly.

"That's where we'll go," she said. "You can walk with us."

I laughed and nodded. Sure, I'd love to. Whistling, I continued on my way.

What a pretty day! The goldenrod along the ditch could not have been yellower, and the flower parts of the thistles as purple as could be. I was not the only one who had thought of a walk this afternoon, those two people had, too. Luxuriously they were strolling along the grassy edge of the road, the sun peeking at them through the trees, making their hair shiny—even the tops of their shoes, where the leather had not cracked.

I was going to sit down right here, in front of our house. As soon as I saw Sini, I'd tell her what had happened. "I talked to a lot of kids," I'd say casually as if this was the fifty-fifth time in a week. And then, when she had already begun to look pleased about that, I'd say, "I think I'm making friends, Sini."

Yep. She was not the only one who was. Me, too. And I had been back only— Let's see . . . six weeks.

Sini had found a job, in a home for children from Winterswijk whose parents had been traitors and were now in jail.

How could she, said the people who gathered at the tree. "A Jewish girl working for *them*? What's the matter with her? Doesn't she know how many of us they helped send to concentration camps?" Their fingers shook as they went down the lists again. "No . . . no. . . . There's not one other Winterswijk name here."

"It was the parents who did those things," Sini protested. "The children are innocent. My God, some of them can't even talk yet, they're so little."

Father and Rachel were glad about Sini. "At last she's doing something useful with her time," they said.

They weren't thinking of those poor children. Not easy having to put up with Sini, six days a week yet. Well, it was fine with me. I was busy. I had lots of things going on.

There was the masseur at four, and the kids I had met. Sometimes when I passed them now, I walked over to them. They smiled, said hello, and the older girl, Jannie, always reminded me that I would be walking to school with them. School—that was another place I went to almost every day, to see whether the soldiers had left and the roof been fixed. Plus I did errands for Rachel. I wouldn't have had much time anyway for what-was-her-name-again, Sini. It was just as well she had a job. But right after I told her so, I turned away. She didn't have to see my face.

· 7 ·

Some nights it rained. I could hear it clattering against my window and on the roof. Bong, bong. The sound of the bell in the church clock was very faint, as if it came from the next town over.

Not Rachel, though. She was loud, night after night, walking around downstairs, talking to herself. "A cow with hoof-and-mouth disease. Fine story. Who does he think he's kidding? And Sini only home to eat, then off again. . . . What am I waiting up for? To let them in? As exhausted as I am. I must be crazy!"

Very loud now. It came from the hall, near the front door. "No more. Let them remember their keys. And if they don't—that's too bad!"

Click, the lock. Through the rain I could hear something else. A dog, barking—not Bobbie.

A week went by. Then one morning Sini did not come down for breakfast. Father ran upstairs to get her. "Sini, get out of bed," he yelled. "You have to go to work."

When he came back downstairs, he said she couldn't. He looked frightened. "I don't understand, Rachel. You go and talk to her. I'm late already."

But Rachel came back downstairs alone too. Sini was exhausted and nauseous was all she said.

Instead of going to work, Father rushed off to town for a doctor. An hour later he returned with one. Anxiously we waited outside Sini's door. When the doctor came out, he said she had jaundice.

"But the vomiting this morning," Father said

nervously. "Are you sure she's not— Go and get the doctor a clean towel, Annie."

I got halfway to the closet. Again the doctor said it was jaundice. "Positively, Mr. de Leeuw." He began to sound irritated.

"If you're sure then—" Father wiped his face. Gratefully he shook the doctor's hand.

All day I tiptoed in and out of Sini's room. "Rachel wants to know what you want." No? No oatmeal? Sini only wanted to sleep? That was all right. I wouldn't force her. I'd be back soon. Maybe then she'd eat.

Sometimes Rachel came, and stayed. Then the three of us talked. Not about cleaning, not about religion—about us. Nights were special, too. Even Father was home, and we all sat by Sini's bed.

"Remember, Father, when she was little," Rachel said, "how she used to stop everyone in the street a few days before her birthday? 'Hey, you, c'mere a minute. See that house over there? 'S mine. In two days I'll be four,' she'd shriek. Two days later perfect strangers would come and ring the bell, Annie, holding a present. 'Give this to the little girl who has a birthday today,' they'd say. 'We think her name is Sini.' Mother would be so ashamed." Rachel was wiping tears from her eyes, from laughing as well as crying.

" 'Sini's not like other people,' your mother used to say." Father got up from his chair and bent over Sini's bed. Clumsily he smoothed her pillow. "Go to sleep now," he said. "It's late. Come on." But his voice was soft, not angry—nice.

July was turning into a wonderful month, and not only at home. "Isn't it amazing," everyone said and looked at the sky with smiles on their faces. "We just can't get over it. We haven't had a summer like this since before the war. Not a cloud— How many days does this make now?" And they'd hurry on, still smiling.

Then it changed. No, not the weather—Sini. Every day she became a little better and stronger, which was good, of course. But she was angry. Almost every time I came upstairs, she began: "Look where I am. In bed, missing out on all the sun. I'm becoming as pale as I used to be. I want to get out." Furiously she sat up. "If that doctor says I have to stay here much longer, I'm sure I'll lose my job. And the soldiers will have been sent home. Then what will I do? Hang around the house day and night? For what?" She flopped back onto the pillow.

Silently I plucked a piece of thread off her blanket. It was an old one. It even had little holes in it.

"And where are Johan and Dientje? Why haven't they visited us this summer?" Sini asked.

That's exactly what I wanted to know. I got up. Slowly I went downstairs, looking I didn't know for what. Maybe I'd keep Rachel company for a while. She was sitting at the kitchen table with three books in front of her, open, every one of them. She was doing her work for the minister, for when she got baptized. For a second she looked up.

"I want you to ask the masseur something," she said.

What! Going once a day was not enough?

"See whether he'll let you ride a bicycle, Annie. And make sure you ask whether you can ride a lot."

What was the matter with Rachel? The only bicycle in the house was Father's, and he was always on it. Crazy people, all three of them. It was all the same again, just as it was before Sini's sickness. She should not have gotten better. There—I slammed the door as I left—that would show them.

· 8 ·

The next morning Rachel called me to come outside. "Hurry up, Annie. I have a surprise for you. You'll never guess what it is."

I rushed out. She was holding a bicycle, with tires that looked almost new, a bell, and just a little bit of rust here and there.

"Do you like it, Annie?"

"Yes." Who was it for? Me?

"Try getting on it, and let me see if it's too high."

No, it was just right. Now what? Confused, I looked at her.

"Would you like to go to Usselo?" she asked.

Did she mean it? "Rachel?" She did. I put my arms around her neck and kissed her. And I had almost not asked the masseur!

"Practice as much as you can," Rachel said, "and on Monday, after the doctor comes to look in on Sini, he'll take you in his car as far as Haaksbergen. He'll let you off there, and you can ride the rest of the way."

"I wish I could go with you."

I looked up. Sini was standing at the window. Well, she couldn't come. She was still a little sick. Besides, Rachel had only borrowed one bicycle— for me.

Carefully, I sat down on the seat. For a second I raised my hand and waved. "Good-bye, Rachel." Slowly I began to move. Look, how I was riding —very straight, nowhere near the trees. Oops, careful, that was a little close. But look now. The road was becoming shorter and shorter . . . behind me already. I raced across the tracks and onto the cobblestones without even slowing down. Too bad the kids weren't there to see me. Maybe later, when I'd be out practicing again.

It was crowded along the main road from Winterswijk to Enschede, even now, this early in the day. There were almost more people on the road than there had been in May.

"Can you take us?" shouted the ones who wanted to go in our direction.

The doctor had to keep shaking his head, no.

I leaned forward. In a couple of hours I'd be there. Sure, it was not that far. Usselo came long before Enschede, and at our speed. . . .

Johan and Dientje would be so surprised to see me, they'd probably think they were dreaming. "Can't be. Our Annie can't have ridden forty kilometers," and they'd rub their eyes and go back to work. I smiled; I couldn't wait.

The car stopped. "This is where I'll let you off," the doctor said.

Haaksbergen already? It had come awfully fast.

"Ready, Annie?"

Sure. I had to laugh myself. I took the bicycle from him.

"Meet me here on Friday, at noon."

"I will." Carefully I studied the house he was walking toward. Then, with my body bent over the handlebars, I took off. I could go fast, too. Just give me a minute until I really get going. Yes, like that. Not bad, right? Almost like a racer. That's what I think. Down, legs, down. C'mon, c'mon, c'mon. Down, down, down, down, past one white stone marker after another that said how much farther to Enschede. Better not forget to subtract all those kilometers for Usselo. Still, that many more to go? Six? After all of this? Maybe I'd take a rest soon. I'll do it right now. Panting, I got off and sank down on the grass. I was going to take it easier after this. Even my head hurt. For a few minutes I lay perfectly still. There, I had started to feel better. Now I could see where I was. A nice spot I had chosen, right by a mass of broom brushes. I touched one of the yellow puffs—silky.

Through half-shut eyes I saw two other people who were sitting nearby jump up and begin their dash to the middle of the road. A car must be coming. Yes. With a screeching sound, it came to a halt.

"Step right in," the driver said, grinning. But he did not mean them. He meant another couple who were strolling toward him from another spot on the grass, a loaf of bread in their hands.

The two people who had reached the car first

but empty-handed began to walk away, complaining that there was no justice.

I checked the watch Sini had let me take. I'd better move on. I got to my feet. Down, and down, and down. Soon I'd be there. Around the next bend, maybe? No, not yet. Then around the next one. . . .

Behind me I could hear horses' hooves, clattering closer, and the sound of wheels. The wagon was loaded high with potato peels. Maybe the man was going to deliver them to the farms in Usselo. Then I had to be very close.

Down, and down. Slowly I pushed my way past another stone marker. Wasn't I there yet? Please! Down, and down, and down.

There was the turn, at last. I could see the farms and a few other buildings, the café, Spieker Diena's dry-goods store, and a little bit of rubble that was still there from the bakery and parsonage. In between and beyond were the fields, one square of yellow after another. Here and there farmers were working in them, cutting the rye. Steadily they swung their arms back and forth; their backs, in the black-and-white striped shirts, bent. They moved their feet carefully so the wooden shoes would not flatten any of the stalks their sickles had not yet reached.

I took a deep breath. I didn't have to look at the

road sign; I knew. I was in Usselo. One more second— Stiffly I got off my bicycle and walked through the gate. Opoe's little garden, beautiful. Behind it was the house, red brick with green trimmings. I stepped over the apples that had fallen into brownish piles and the swarming wasps that were buzzing around them and digging in. If I wanted to, I could close my eyes, keep them closed, and know exactly what I would see: milk jugs, four of them, waiting to be used, right outside the kitchen door; the tree that grew practically against the wall of the house, the—*ssht*, don't get so excited—windows with white curtains, the begonia plants on saucers. Remember me, all of you? I'm back. No, not to hide— to *visit!*

Well, let's see. No point going into the house at this hour, but someone would be out by the chicken coop. Laughing softly, I tiptoed over. Sure, someone was—Opoe! But who was that ugly fat dog that was walking next to her? What was he doing here? Maybe he did not belong.

I ran the last few feet. "Opoe, look who's here!"

Her face wrinkled up with laughter. "God-o-god-o-god, that could be our Annie."

"Opoe, it is."

"Isn't that something? You came all by yourself!" She stepped back to look at me. "My Annie.

I'd better get busy right away. You must be hungry —and thirsty, I bet. Sure, after such a trip. Fui-fui." She rushed off to the kitchen, followed by the dog. "Stop barking, Vlekje. She's family."

I approached the stable. There were two people inside. I threw open the door and marched in. They heard nothing. They saw nothing either. Not now, no. Carefully I took another step—

"Goddammit, Dientje, look!" Johan shouted and dropped the pail he was holding. "That's our little Annie."

"Johan, what's the matter with you?" Dientje shrieked. "Let go. You're crushing her. Johan!"

But her hug was just as hard. At last she let me go.

"We would've come to see you, Annie. You and Sini weren't mad, were you?" They looked at me. Something had happened to Dientje's knee, Johan explained. "She fell and hurt it. We tried getting her on the bike a couple of times, but she couldn't get going."

The kitchen was busy. Johan was washing his face at the pump, splashing water on everything— the dog that was still there, the wooden shoes lined up by the door.

"Watch what you're doing," Dientje screamed

from in front of the stove. "I'm standing right where I get it." But she was laughing, like Opoe and me.

"Hey, Annie, did I ever show you how well Ma can dance? Ha, ha, Ma, look at Annie's face; she doesn't believe me. C'mon, just you and me." He pulled Opoe off the chair. "How d'you like it, Annie, eh? It's a waltz."

"Johan, what's the matter with you? My legs won't go."

"Nonsense, Ma. You're doing fine for an old woman." And he kept on singing and taking back-and-forth waltz steps in his socks, while all the time trying to keep them out of the dog's mouth.

"Fui-fui." Opoe laughed. "That Johan. He's so happy you're here, Annie. He hasn't acted this way since you left."

I hadn't either. I was rocking back and forth in Opoe's easy chair, doing a little dance of my own. Listen to Johan; he was yodeling now. A waltz, too? I kept still for a minute to think. Yes, it was. There, I began rocking again.

But Dientje had had enough. "Stop acting up, Johan," she yelled. "You're giving me a headache, and it isn't even noon yet."

"That late?" Opoe looked shocked. She sat down and pulled a basket of potatoes onto her lap. The dog immediately curled up against her legs.

"What d'you think of him, Annie?" Johan asked.

"Very cute," I said. But was the dog staying with them forever? Yes, he was. That's what Johan was telling me.

"Opoe was so homesick for you. 'Where's that giggly one,' she kept asking. Right, Ma? All the time. It got so bad, Annie, we had to get her a dog."

"Ja, ja. But it's not the same thing, Johan," Opoe protested.

That made me laugh again. Of course, it was not.

In front of a rusty piece of mirror, Johan was combing his hair. It wouldn't stay flat. It kept springing up like brown and gray rubber bands. He must have been out in the sun a lot, for his face was very red, especially his nose and ears.

"Well, that's that. A handsome man you're looking at, Annie. What d'you say, eh?"

"Yes, Johan." He was. He liked my answer. He smiled a few times at himself before he hung the mirror on the nail again.

With a long enamel spoon Dientje was stirring something in a pan. Billows of steam were coming up, enveloping her, then thinning out and spreading until they hit the window, the door, the tiled walls, becoming drops that ran down and formed tiny puddles on the stone floor. So many wonderful sounds here: the flames racing across the wood in the stove, the teakettle whistling, the potatoes plopping into the bucket, the scraping of Johan's chair as he pulled it up right next to mine.

"Now tell me what's happening in Winterswijk."

Intently they listened. Once in a while they would say something. "That Sini, she's got it in her, Johan. I could tell when she was dancing here. Those feet couldn't stay still." "But that was Liberation Day. Every night now? No, that's not right for a young girl. No wonder she got sick. And then complaining, too! Fui-fui!"

From Sini, I went on to Rachel, and again they listened and had things to say.

"What? To church twice on Sundays?" Johan could hardly believe it. "I'll be damned. Here, Dientje, goes once a year, and that's only because of the neighbors."

"New Year's Eve, Annie. I never skip. You know that."

With her lips pursed, Opoe said she'd love to go all the time if it weren't for her lace cap. "It's too much work to put on, Annie, and without it, it doesn't look right. But that's the only reason. Does Rachel talk religious, too?" she wanted to know. "Because some of 'em do when they get that way,

like old woman Roerink who always says—ah—"
Opoe had trouble remembering. "The morning
may—ah, ah—be beautiful, but we never know
what ah—" She puckered up her forehead. "—the
night will bring us," she finished. With a sigh of
relief, she began on another potato.

And I told them that every day I had to go to the
masseur, that I was tired of it.

"She shouldn't have to, Johan," Opoe said
firmly. "There's nothing wrong with her legs. A
little short and crooked, but that's the way they
grew. You're a pretty girl, Annie. What did you
call that man? Ah, I can't even say it. Pooh, what
does he know."

"Annie"—I looked at Johan. His face was serious—"I'll tell you something. You should've stayed
here for always and not gone back to Winterswijk.
I don't even care for the town from what I saw. I
guess I had it pictured wrong in my head. It's not
cozy."

"We sure would've liked you to stay." Shyly
Dientje looked at me. "We wanted to ask your
father when he came to pick you up, but we didn't
have the heart. He was so glad to see you. It
would've been nice though, Annie, what?"

Vigorously I nodded my head.

"But I'm still kind of a mother to you, right?"

"Of course, Dientje."

With a pleased smile she moved the spoon around in the pan again.

"We've got a school here, too," Johan went on proudly. "You should see, a room as big as a house, Annie. With desks, nice pots of ink in the middle, everything. And I could've seen you every time I went by with the horse." He laughed just thinking about it.

So did I. "Excuse me," I'd say to the teacher when I heard trotting noises, "I'd like to look out the window a minute." And I'd run, wave. "Hi, Johan."

"And don't think we haven't got soldiers here for Sini. Ha, ha, plenty."

Well, that I didn't like.

"We've even got 'em visiting us. Ja, ja, I'm not kidding. Last week one walked right into the kitchen. Awfully nice fellow. We talked a lot."

"You didn't." Dientje laughed through the steam.

Johan ignored her. "He stood around for a minute and said something like Borrow-horse-cart. 'Well, my name's a lot easier,' I said. 'Just call me Johan.' We both kept on saying the same thing, Annie. After a while I gave him an egg. Had to get rid of him somehow."

"Ah, Johan, he must've come for something else. He looked so confused."

"Then he should've said what he came for. He left with the egg though. He even gave me a little tobacco, he was so happy." Johan pointed at the cigarette in his hand. "Here, this is one of 'em. How many farmers in Usselo do you think he could have had a conversation with in English, eh?" Triumphantly he blew a mouthful of smoke at the stove where it merged with the clouds of steam. "No one. That Sini was a good English teacher."

"Fui-fui," Opoe complained. "It's becoming harder and harder to see here." She took off her glasses and rubbed them against her apron. "Johan—" Her voice was urgent. She half got off her chair. "I hear someone coming. Annie, upstairs. Quick, quick. Johan, make'r go. *Joha-a-an.*"

We stared at her. "The war's over."

"Ah, ja. What's the matter with me? Ashamed, Opoe put her hand in front of her mouth. "It must've been my imagination."

"Well, woman," Johan yelled, holding his fork up. "I'm ready to give you your dinner."

"Just a minute." Dientje tried to see into the pan, frowned, gave the stew a stir anyway, and lifted the pan from the stove. "All right, Johan. Hurry up. Make some space on the table. Don't wait; it's heavy." Groaning, she set the pan down in the middle of the table.

With his fork Johan began to mark off portions. "Ma, this little strip by the handle is yours. Dientje, boy, look at what I'm letting you have, almost as much as me. Ha, ha. Don't worry, Ma. I won't forget about our Annie. This nice little pile is all for her."

I pushed my chair closer to the table, picked up my fork, and dug in. Three big flies buzzed up and down the table, trying to find a way into the pan. I slapped at them. Go away.

Vlekje was standing on his hind legs, his paws on Opoe's arm. But Dientje wouldn't let Opoe give him anything. "Don't forget, Mother, he's only a dog."

A nice dog though. Sweet eyes. And the steam . . . it made everything even more cozy. All wrapped up—us. Contentedly I licked my fork.

"It's good, Annie, isn't it? Nice and crusty, the meat, right? The way you like it?" Dientje asked.

With my mouth full I answered, "Yes." Her whole face beamed.

We had finished eating. The flies had dived into the pan and were walking across the bottom. Johan tipped his chair back, stuck out his legs, and pulled a red handkerchief from his pocket to wipe his mouth.

"Dientje, after you've cleaned up here, I want you to lie down for a while. Ja, ja, take a rest. You look awfully tired. It must be the knee. It'll do it good."

"What?" With big eyes Dientje stared at him. "I don't understand. All you've done for weeks is complain about my resting. You told me my knee was all better now."

He ignored her. "And, Ma, you do the same. Off to bed with the two of you."

"I won't sleep, Johan," Opoe protested. "And I've got to put fresh straw down for the chickens."

"I don't care. Let them use the old stuff. We're all going to have a little what-d'you-call-it—vacation. C'mon, Annie."

"Where are you going?" Dientje asked.

"To the front of the house, woman."

"But Johan, this morning you said you had so much to do that we wouldn't see you till dark. Now look at you."

"Ah, Dientje, that was this morning. C'mon, Annie."

I followed Johan out of the kitchen.

"Ja, ja, Annie, life's not easy." Johan sat down between the geranium beds in front of the house, his arms resting on his legs. "We've had nothing but trouble the last couple of months. First Opoe with the head. Then Dientje with the leg. All I've done is work, Annie. I bet that's what has kept me healthy. Remember, during the war Dientje and Ma always had to push me? 'Go, Johan, what's the matter with you? You can't stay in the house all day. The grass, the turnips. . . .' No more. I run to work. What's there to stay home for now that you and Sini are gone?"

I took his hand. We sat close, saying nothing. When he began to talk again, he sounded more cheerful. "But you never know, Annie. You could come back and live here. Crazy things happen. Who would've thought you'd come here in the first place? Eh?" In front of us a butterfly kept waltzing by, its yellow wings glistening in the sun.

The sounds of footsteps came from the road. I could see a farmer, a sickle across his shoulder. "Afternoon, Piet," Johan called out to him. "How goes?"

"That's Annie," Piet shouted, running over. "I was talking about you just a few minutes ago. Ja, ja, we still can't get over it. I was telling the wife's cousin how I thought I wasn't seeing right when you first hobbled out of the house in April. Who's that? I asked everyone, but they didn't know, either. That Johan, how he kept it hidden from us! And that's not easy in Usselo, Annie—let me tell you. Here, we even thought Johan was crazy, never getting into the air-raid shelter with the rest of us," Piet said, shaking his head.

"I was home with the girls, Piet, under the table. I always said if a bomb hits the house I might just as well get killed with them. You should've seen Annie—trembled like a leaf." Johan squeezed my hand. "Eh? How could I have left her?"

"I'm telling you, Annie. That Johan is something."

"Listen to him talk," Johan said modestly.

"Well"—Piet put his sickle over his other shoulder—"I've got to begin cutting the rye, Johan. Koos has most of his down already, and you hate to be the last one. If you ask me, this weather can't go on forever."

Behind us someone was knocking loudly on the window. "Johan, Johan"—I could see Dientje's head through the curtains—"get off the grass. What's the matter with you, sitting there in broad daylight? No one else in Usselo is doing it, I'll bet. What'll people think?"

"Ahh—" But Johan got up. 'C'mon, Annie. We'd better get going."

I followed them all afternoon, ducking first into the chicken coop where Opoe was. "That one, Annie, with the funny eyes, always takes her own time. I have to keep reminding her what she's sitting there for. Come, chickie, I haven't got all afternoon."

Vlekje was curled up in the corner, his paws on a layer of peat litter. "Quiet, Annie." Opoe put her finger against her lips. "There, she's doing it." Opoe sounded relieved. A minute later she rushed over to the nest. "I've got to be quick with this one. She likes to eat the shell. She doesn't want to wait till it's empty, and I feed it to her. C'mon, get off now."

The chicken got up, turned around to see what she had done, looked again. Then, cackling angrily, she left the coop.

"Nice egg, Annie. She got it a little dirty, but I'll wash it. You're going to have it for supper tonight." With a damp rag Opoe carefully cleaned the egg.

In the kitchen where steam was still rising and dripping again, Dientje and a neighbor were canning beans. They snipped off the ends, broke them in two, threw them into a pot, and took up new ones from the heap in their laps.

"You want anything, Annie? An apple maybe?" Dientje asked. "Shall I get you one from the side of the house? No? A cookie? One with sugar sprinkles? She likes those, Leida."

"Ha-ha, ha-ha," Leida laughed.

I couldn't take my eyes off her. Everything made her laugh, even when Dientje asked, "How many jars d' you think this will make?" She must have seen me looking at her.

"I bet Annie wonders what's the matter with me." Leida laughed again. "No teeth. I had 'em all pulled, Annie. All of a sudden I had such a toothache." She showed me where. "Couldn't sleep, couldn't work, it hurt so. I went to the dentist, and I said, 'Out with 'em. I've had enough of pain in the mouth.' Now I'm getting some new ones"—she giggled—"in a couple of weeks, for my thirty-fifth birthday. Some dentist in the city, Dientje, who first asked for a hundred guilders and a dozen eggs, but after I sat down in the chair and he had gotten the last ones out, he wanted more. Now I can't get the new ones from him for less than four dozen, which isn't very nice of him." Laughing, she closed another jar.

"Ja, ja, Leida. The war made a lot of people bad," Dientje agreed. One by one, she lowered the jars into the boiling water.

Johan was in the stable, sitting next to the only cow that was in there. "I've got to keep a close eye on her, Annie. She's had a lot of trouble before when she's calved." He stroked her sides. "Ja. Better not be in the middle of the night again, you hear? Not like the other time." He lifted his cap and scratched his head. "Too bad I can't tell for sure whether it's going to be a boy or girl calf, Annie. Some farmers tie a golden ring to a piece of string and let it dangle. If it turns one way, it means a boy calf; the other way, a girl. But I for one"—he scratched the cow's head, too—"don't believe in such nonsense. I say she's been awfully jumpy for a day or two, so it's going to be a girl. And, Annie, listen to this. I'm going to give her a special name. Guess what one." He laughed mysteriously.

"I can't, Johan."

"Want me to tell you? It's going to be Annie. This way there'll be an Annie around here all the time. In the meadow, in the stable, 'Annie,' I'll yell, and she'll be right there! What d'you think of that, eh?"

Calves were cute. They had big ears and such long legs. I liked it, I told him.

"I thought you would. Ja, ja, leave it to Johan. Hey, where are you off to now?"

The chicken coop, of course. I didn't want to miss a thing that was going on.

It was getting to be evening. The sun was going down red, turning the whole sky that color and a little purple, too, all the way down to the trees.

Bunches of flies danced around in clusters, landing sometimes, but mostly not. A rooster crowed. I leaned against the gate, close to where Johan had tied up the four cows to be milked. Their backs were covered with pieces of canvas. From time to time they shook their heads and swept their tails around to chase away the flies. For a second it helped. Milk began to splash and hiss into the pails as Johan and Dientje's hands moved the teats up and down.

"Getting tired, Annie?"

"Just a little, Dientje." But it was a nice kind of tired, a peaceful kind. From the gate I heard their voices again, hushed. They were talking about tomorrow.

"We can't wait another day with the rye, Johan, or we'll be the only ones with ours still up."

"First thing tomorrow, after the calf. Make a batch of pancake sandwiches, something to drink, blanket for Annie to sit on—"

"Not too close to the sickle, Johan."

"I know, woman, what d'you take me for?"

"And we'll bring a straw hat, Johan. We don't want her to get sunburned."

"Maybe we can find her one of those white aprons, like Ma used to wear."

I was having such a good time already, just listening. Tomorrow, the day after, the one after that, and then— No, I didn't want to think about that day now. I scratched my arms. There were an awful lot of flies around; that, I didn't like.

Johan had finished with his cow. He emptied the pail into the jug. Steaming, the milk rushed through the strainer, leaving foam that fizzed around, then slowly dissolved. The sky was becoming a little darker, less red. Soon we'd all be sitting in the kitchen with the door open, to let in the last of the light. Opoe was already there, cutting bread for supper. She'd hold the loaf against her bosom and carve. Just before the knife touched the apron, she'd stop and break the slice off. A minute later she'd add a piece of wood to the stove, so the water would boil for tea—and my egg. She'd take four knives from the drawer, wipe the oilcloth on the table, get out the cups. . . .

Noiselessly I left the gate. I had to go inside and see for myself.

The four days were over. They had gone so fast I felt as if I had just come. Johan's rye was still not all gathered into sheaves. I could have gone to the fields again with him and Dientje, woven another basket, picked more cornflowers, selected more straws for binding the rye.

Slowly I pedaled away.

Far behind me, from the stable, came mooing sounds. The cow had calved—a girl. "Did just as I told her," Johan had said. And we had laughed. Closer, I could hear voices, three of them, calling good-bye, telling me to be careful, to say hello to Sini, Rachel, Father, and to come back. Then I could no longer hear them. But when I turned around to look, they were still there.

The fields again, practically bare now. A few birds were flying over the stubble, looking for spilled grain. When they saw a kernel, they swooped down, pecked at it. Flapping wings against the gray sky, the only sounds. Last field . . . the turn.

Funny, I had not said anything to them about Father, that he was always out. Not on business either, Rachel said, not at night, not when it was pitch-dark. "How could he see?" Besides, he wouldn't take a bath every day, she said, not for cows. Where did he go then?

· 9 ·

"I think I'm all set." Sini picked up her bag and looked around the room to make sure she had left nothing behind. She turned to Father and Rachel.

"I'll be fine," she assured them again. "Don't worry." Quickly she ran down the stairs. I followed her. A second later we closed the back door behind us.

Already we were halfway to the railroad crossing, but the gate was down. Good. A freight train was coming. Noisily the two cars sped by. We crossed the tracks. Did Sini notice how fancy the Misterstraat looked compared to when we first came home? Pieces of glass taken from picture frames had been installed in the boards across the store windows, some so large that several people could see in at once. And read the signs that said what you could buy now and what would be coming soon. Or, as in the shoestore, see a real shoe. But, no, Sini was in too much of a hurry to get to that city she was going to, to become a nurse—Enschede, where so much was happening that she wouldn't know what to choose from first. Listen to her carry on. The minute I got out of bed this morning, she began again, just as she had yesterday and the day before.

"Three movie houses, not only Fred Astaire all week as you have here. Concerts, restaurants . . . close to Johan and Dientje . . . lots of places to go to dance. . . . I'm so excited."

We passed the marketplace, and on the left, that

café. The sign "Nightly Dances" was gone, pulled down by the proprietor the day the Canadian soldiers left. "Thank God," people had said, "at last we can get a good night's sleep again. All that noise. . . ."

How could they have thought that? It had been music, pleasant music. They should have stayed, those soldiers. Then maybe Sini would have, too.

"Come on, Annie."

Yes, yes, I was trying to walk fast.

"Let's wait here."

We had reached the edge of town. And it had taken us hardly any time.

Sini pulled a mirror from her bag. She looked closely at her face, dabbing at the lipstick a soldier had given her. Rachel had been upset by the lipstick. It was sinful, she said; if God had wanted Sini to have such red lips, He would have made them that way. But to me it looked beautiful. The first car that comes along will surely stop for her, I thought.

"Well, do you think I look all right for the big city, Annie?"

"Yes."

With her arm around my shoulder we waited, not talking. A motorcycle went by with two passengers squeezed into the back seat. No cars. Once or twice Sini went to the middle of the road, just to look. If none came by dark, we'd have to turn around whether she wanted to or not. Go home . . . unpack. . . .

Numbly I heard truck sounds and saw Sini signal. I stared at the ground. A mail truck was slowing down.

"Good-bye, Annie." Sini's voice was hoarse. "I can't stay with you forever. I have to get out of this town. It's dead for me. Rachel cares a lot about you, Annie. You'll be fine, better even."

Of course. Of course. Stubbly grass we were standing on; I could almost feel it through my shoes. She kissed me. Then walked to the truck.

The people in the back pulled her up. "You'll love it here," they said to her, laughing. "Nice canvas armchairs, compliments of the government." With a plop, she landed on a mailbag.

"Okay?" The driver stuck his head out the window. "Then let's go." More laughter as everyone bounced around.

My eyes followed the truck. She'd wave, wouldn't she? Not forget I was still here? Someone half stood up, crawled to the tailgate; a hand moved back and forth, Sini's. Mine did, too.

Suddenly a streetlamp went on. "Got it to

work," a repairman said, grinning. The very first one. Could Sini see it? Well, what difference would it make if she did? None. She would still have said there were more lights in Enschede. I wiped my eyes. It's just that we had been close for so long.

· *10* ·

On the island of Walcheren thousands of men were working very hard, yet not one hole in the dikes had been closed. Anxiously they counted the number of days till November, when the winter storms could rip apart whatever had been repaired. "Less than eighty days," they said worriedly, and picked up even bigger loads of rocks and sand and clay, ignoring the rain that had been coming down on them for days now.

"Didn't I tell you the weather we were having was abnormal?" people all over Holland said as they hurried through the streets in waterlogged shoes—or carried them tucked under their arms since no shoe coupons had been issued yet. When they reached the stores, they always found the same long lines of people, no matter how early they arrived. Wet, too, and irritable about many things —the weather, housing, food.

"I still come home with the same cabbage and beans. My husband said one more meal like that, and he's moving out."

"Where to?" a woman with an umbrella answered. "The government isn't building any housing yet. They don't even do repairs. Our roof is still leaking. We had to move the beds to the kitchen!"

"This is what I want to know. Why do sick people get extra food coupons, whereas healthy people are the ones with appetites?" The man hitched up his pants before he stated his next complaint. "And those refugees. The minister got us to take one in. It'll be ten months tomorrow. Where's the end? The only good thing that's happened lately is that the newspaper is back, even if it's only two pages long. At least I can sit down with the news again and go over it as often as I want to."

Holding my purchases under my sweater, I crossed the street. What was so good about newspapers? Nothing. They had ads from all over— hospital ones. "We need you," they said in big letters. "Thousands and thousands of sick people are waiting. We can't accept them unless you become a nurse." I kicked a stone hard. Good, it splashed right into a puddle.

At the tree in the marketplace, the people who came to read the notices were irritable, too. "Why hasn't the man from Town Hall come anyway?" they complained. "Today's his day. Just because of the rain! *We* are here." But their voices sounded a little relieved.

He came a few days later, carrying the new list. It was a longer one this time. Stiffly people approached the tree, looking for the same names they had been hoping to find all these months: Emma Cohen, Meier Philips, Herman Schaap, Mozes Spier, Jakob Vos—all the relatives and friends they had known, who had ended up in those camps with odd-sounding names. Auschwitz, Dachau, Bergen-Belsen, others.

Again they did not find them. When they got to the end of the list, they saw what was printed on the last line. "COMPLETE," it read. "ANYONE ELSE SHOULD BE CONSIDERED DEAD."

Mrs. Vos, the woman with the pretty brown hair, clutched the arm of her daughter. Like the others, they were crying.

Slowly the area around the tree emptied out. The farmers who still had flowers left to sell picked them up and put them in their carts—dahlias, chrysanthemums, marigolds, their orange heads barely sticking up over the rims of the pails. "If we're lucky, we'll get home before it gets any windier," the farmers called out to each other.

I was going home, too. None of my friends'

names had been on that list either, and not one of Father's ten brothers and sisters.

· *11* ·

Rachel seemed to have changed. In the morning she still enumerated all the chores that had to be done that day: "The windows, the kitchen floor, the living-room chairs." But she did not mean all day, not any more. After a few hours, she'd say, "Let's take a break," just like that. She'd offer me her arm. I'd take it. And off we'd go.

Sometimes we visited Maria, at the end of the road. On the way we'd stop and say hello to the neighbors—the Ten Riets, Mulders, and Geerdeses —but we'd hurry past the Droppers. Or, we'd go in the opposite direction—toward town—to Mrs. Menko's house, and sit by her chair. Had she gained any weight since last week? we'd ask.

"A pound, the doctor told me."

"Beautiful, Mrs. Menko, but it should be more." She'd smile, tell Rachel not to worry. "I'm even walking around the house again, and my hair is growing back a little," she'd say. "Look." And she'd lift her kerchief, to show us.

We were not the only ones who visited her.

Others tiptoed in, too, strangers even, bringing something for her to eat—an egg, a cup of milk, a mouthful of meat—the same way Rachel and I did. They'd put it down on the table. "Don't say no, Mrs. Menko. We can spare it," they'd say softly, in case her head was hurting again.

"Aren't people wonderful," she said, wiping her eyes. But carefully, for they hurt, too.

We did other things, Rachel and I. We went to all the stores. Take today. We had already stood in line for a long time, and not to buy either, just to look through the openings in the boards. The mannequin in De Wind's Mode had her sheet off for the first time. There were real clothes on her now —not ordinary boring ones, either. A slip to her knees, and a bracelet on each wrist. "Isn't she beautiful, Rachel?" I said, straining to stand even higher on my toes.

"She could use a tweed suit," Rachel said, "to go over everything."

"Yes, with a fur collar." Definitely, soft on the chin.

"And a hat, Annie. One that sits straight on the head."

"With a ribbon—"

"Walking shoes—"

"Gloves, Rachel—all the way to the elbow."

It had been wonderful outfitting her, and having talked so long about clothes had given Rachel an idea. I was going to get a jacket, a maroon one, she decided. No, not from De Wind's Mode. They had nothing but underwear yet. Rachel was going to make me one out of a drapery. Soon, she said, so I'd have it before the winter and could wear it to school.

"Well." Rachel laughed. "Have a good time exercising, and I'll see you in an hour."

"I will," I said, laughing, too. Rachel was almost the way she used to be—fun.

I skipped down the Misterstraat and into another street where the sidewalk was so narrow that you almost had to be an acrobat not to fall off. There. Perfect. Right up to the masseur's door.

One thing had not changed, though, about Rachel. Every night she still sat down with the same books—the Bible and those others with the lessons for her baptism. Even now that the library was open again. The praying and the churchgoing, that had not changed, either. A few other Jews in town had come back Christians just as religious as she, but they had already given it up. "Wore off with them after a couple of weeks," Father said, and he sounded envious.

Wasn't Rachel getting tired of it, too? Should I ask her? Or would she get angry with me, as she had with Father.

"Rachel?"

Her face became very red, but it was not from anger. "Without the Christian religion I would not have survived the war. And I'm not dropping it simply because *that's* over."

I nodded. What did she mean? She said so much that evening, Rachel. "I went to church for the first time during the war. It was Christmas. That's a very special day, Annie, which is why the people who hid me wanted me to go with them. Weeks before they told everyone in church that a cousin would be coming to visit for the holidays. I had not left my room for a year. I was so afraid. How would it feel to be outside again? That was all I thought about. And snow was coming down on Christmas day—I walked in it. I thought everyone was looking at me. Not that they could have seen much; my black hair was hidden under a red kerchief. They couldn't know I was Jewish. So many people were going into the church, it made me dizzy. Quickly my 'family' and I sat down in the back.

"The minister talked about the birth of Christ, about his life, and what it meant. I never knew any of that before. Then the organ began to play, Annie. First so softly I could hardly hear it. But then, all around me, there was music. Louder and louder, until I no longer knew where it came from or where I was. With one foot in heaven, I thought. It was so beautiful.

"When I went back to my room, there was still that music. I never got it out of my head. Almost all year long I could hear it.

"They took me again, the next Christmas. 'Remember that cousin from the city?' my 'family' told everyone. 'She'll be back for her annual visit. We'll be bringing her to church.' I was counting the days, Annie. It was the only thing that made staying in the room the rest of the year bearable."

She stopped. With an embarrassed look, she picked up the Bible again. It was still open to her favorite part, the Gospel according to Saint Matthew.

I stuck out my hand to Rachel. After all, what was so bad about it? Why did it make Father so angry? I'd surprise Rachel on Sunday. I'd wait right outside the church door, maybe even take a look inside for myself. Ask her if she had liked the sermon, walk home with her. I bent my head over my book. We both read. Once in a while we'd stop, look at each other, smile—just for a second, but long enough.

· 12 ·

When we came back on that Sunday afternoon, Father's bicycle was standing by the house. Funny, he had come home already; it wasn't even dark yet. But there was a reason. He had something to tell us, he said. He paced back and forth in the kitchen, taking off his glasses, wiping them on his handkerchief, putting them on again. Finally, "I want you to meet someone." Without looking at us, he said, "My wife-to-be."

"Who?" Maybe I had heard wrong. That could be. But he said them again, the same words, "My wife-to-be." Then, "Rachel, please be nice. It's not easy for her," and bolted out the door.

I rubbed my arms. They felt cold. Rachel pulled me onto her lap. Time went by—not much. I heard voices—Father's and a woman's. Hers was smooth, kind of sharp, though. I knew it, had heard it before, at the marketplace. Mrs. Vos.

She was not alone. The daughter had come, too. Her name was Nel. As Rachel poured tea, and Father and Mrs. Vos talked, I stared at the daughter. She was older than I was, perhaps five or six years. She looked like her mother. The same brown hair, too. Wavy. I searched Nel's face. There had to be something about it that was ugly, but where?

I tucked my legs even farther under the chair. Where? I sighed with relief. She had a tiny wart under her chin.

"It's not a bad house," Mrs. Vos was admitting to Father. "I must say I'm surprised. It's bigger inside than it looks." She turned to Nel. "Don't you think it's a little roomier than ours?"

"But it's so far from town," Nel complained. "It might just as well be in Siberia." That wart wasn't so little. "There's not even a streetlight out here. You won't see a soul this winter—mark my words."

Mrs. Vos nodded pensively. "Yes, you may be right." She examined the plush chair she was sitting on.

"We had much more furniture," Father apologized. "A table, of course, and"—he pointed to the corner—"bookcases." He showed Mrs. Vos the other places in the living room where things used to be. "A clock, a piano along that wall."

"Mother used to play the piano all the time," Rachel said. When no one answered her, she added, "Very well."

I nodded at her. Yes.

"You need talent to play," Mrs. Vos said. With one eyebrow raised, she looked as if she thought Mother could not possibly have had any. Wasn't Father going to say anything? No, he was just listening. "I don't understand how you can have been so dumb, Ies. I got everything back that I stored. You must have left your furniture with very dishonest people. Well," she said in a comforting tone to Father, "if the other things were like these chairs, it's just as well. I won't say anything about the quality, Ies. That's probably not bad, but how old-fashioned can furniture get? People have not sat on stiff chairs like these for years and years."

"They certainly haven't." Nel laughed, shifting to the edge of hers. "Or if they have, I can see why they stopped."

Big teeth—practically like a beaver's.

Mrs. Vos drank the rest of her tea and handed the cup to Rachel. "You know, Ies," she concluded, "as hard as I've looked, I can't see much here that will go with what I have."

Father shrugged his shoulders. "Let me try to sell this stuff then," he suggested. "I don't care."

That should be easy, Mrs. Vos said immediately. Father knew so many farmers, and for them it would be just fine—exactly their taste. She got up and walked around, trying to decide where her own furniture would go. "It will make a big difference, you'll see. This whole place will be transformed into something you won't recognize." She smiled at Rachel. She got no response.

Anxiously Father wiped his forehead. "C'mon,

Magda, Nel. I'll take you home before it gets dark."

We shook hands. She hoped she'd see us again soon. In the door she turned and pinched my cheek. "Good-bye," I mumbled.

Silently Rachel collected the empty teacups, the odds and ends that didn't even match. Mrs. Vos would not want those either, I guessed. She had her own—beautiful ones, no doubt—porcelain or crystal, for all I knew. From China or wherever crystal came from. Should I tell Rachel what Mrs. Vos had said about my legs that time? No, better not. Why hadn't her husband's name appeared on any of those lists from Town Hall. Why not? Jakob Vos. She had gotten everything else back.

· *13* ·

It was a week later that Rachel left, to live again with the people who had hidden her during the war. "Winterswijk does not have any job opportunities, Annie," she said. "Besides, the trains are running again. I'd be a fool not to take advantage of that. I haven't been on one for years! Especially now. The heather's still in bloom; I'll be able to see it just by looking out the window!

But I knew better. I'd heard them when I was upstairs and they didn't know I was listening—Rachel and Father. Rachel must leave, Father had told her. It would never work, he said, she and Mrs. Vos together in the same house. Rachel was only ten years younger—that was why.

"You're twenty-nine years old, and you've seen so little of the world. I would have told you that one of these days anyway. It's not right for you to stay here and take care of Annie and me. You ought to lead your own life with people your own age. Why don't you go to Amsterdam, The Hague . . . or Rotterdam? They're going to rebuild Rotterdam beautifully, I read. You can get a job. You still have your teacher's certificate." He told her to leave. Just like that.

But Rachel had not wanted to move to one of those cities where she knew no one. "I'll go back to my 'family,'" she said.

That upset Father. "Don't, Rachel," he told her. "You'll be taking a step back, not forward. That little town has nothing to offer you. There's just a church there!"

But no matter what Father said, Rachel would not change her mind. She chose to leave on the afternoon train. Father came home early to take her to the station. Silently we walked down the road,

Father in front carrying Rachel's suitcase with her few clothes and the plaques with the religious sayings. Coming toward us was Droppers. He was pushing a wheelbarrow. When he was practically next to us, he looked for a second at the suitcase, then at the three of us. Hopefully, as if he thought we'd all be leaving.

When we reached the station, the train was already there. Rachel rushed right on. She did not look back or come to the window, not even when the train began to go.

I wanted to run along the platform, tell her things loudly so she'd hear me. Tell her I knew she had not wanted to leave, that I hated Mrs. Vos—and Father—that I was just getting to know her, Rachel.

"Come, Annie."

I could still hear the sound of the train.

"Let's not stand around any longer." Father tried to take my hand.

Reluctantly I followed him off the platform. Still, I could hear the train. . . .

Father was waiting for me in front of the station. "The next few days will be difficult, Annie. But remember, we're beginning a whole new life, you and I." He looked at me pleadingly.

What was wrong with the way it had been? Nothing. I buttoned my jacket. Rachel had finished making it right before she left, even though she had been tired.

"You need a mother, Annie, not just sisters."

Sini and Rachel had been like mothers, cared about me. Hadn't Sini always come in to check on me at night even though it was late? And Rachel. . . .

"You'll have no trouble getting along with Magda," Father was saying. "She's a smart woman, and understanding. She had a stepmother herself, so she knows what it's like. And she's had experience with girls."

Yes, with her own daughter, not with me.

"Come, Annie." Father held out his bicycle. "We'll go to Magda's house. She can use some help packing."

I shook my head.

"Where will you go then?"

"Home," I said.

"You'll be all right?"

"Sure." I smiled. I did not need them.

"Maybe later then you can help, when we get to the house."

What would I help with? Taking the furniture out of our living room? I did not even answer. I turned around, left him there.

When I got home, I went into the kitchen. In the meadow across the road a couple of sparrows circled around and around a pail, then landed on the edge of it. There had been a sheep in the meadow the first evening, drinking from the same pail. And Father had said, "I'm a happy man," because we were back, Sini, Rachel, me.

Slowly I walked into the living room, to the little chest with the brown-and-black-striped tea cozy on it. In the middle of the room were the chairs, the ones Mother had liked so.

I pulled one closer, touched it. Prickly. I spread my jacket on the seat, so that it hung down over the edge. I sat down; it was perfect this way. Mother had been right. Quickly I got up, putting the chair back exactly where it had been. I checked the time. Maybe I should sit on the sofa, wait there. It was comfortable. Too bad we'd have to get rid of that, too. I curled up on it.

What was that noise, the doorbell? Quickly I raised my head. No. I lay down again. Rachel was still on the train and would be for another hour. She'd arrive in time to join her "family" and the other families in town on the benches along the canal for their evening chat. Sini might be taking patients' temperatures right now. Or giving them their peanut-butter snack, to make them stronger. Or she could be washing dishes. She could even be with Johan and Dientje—who was like a mother, too. . . .

Now what was that? The bell? Nervously I listened. No, it was the wind, rustling leaves across our gravel path. Summer was over. School next week, at last. I turned on my back and closed my eyes.

Dark all around me, and I was sinking in it, deeper, deeper. What was that? Footsteps? Coming from the road? Boots? Yes, loud ones. Soldiers' boots. Coming straight toward the house, stepping high like toy soldiers, only real. German soldiers. They knocked down the door, stormed in, marching and stamping and shouting to the rhythm of their boots. *Eins, zwei. Eins, zwei.* Bayonets, aimed at me. A hatchet, too, in Droppers' hands. Where was Sini? Rachel? Father? No one answered. *Eins, zwei.* I turned my head, saw a closet. I tried to get up, run into it, but something kept pushing me down. Blackness. Or boots, what? Tried . . . *eins* . . . tried . . . *zwei* . . . couldn't. "Johan," I screamed, "help. *Joha-a-a-a-a-a—*"

I woke up, shaking. I had had this terrible dream, and no one had been there, not even Johan.

A while later, I heard the rattling of a cart. I rushed to the door. Yes, yes, it was stopping, in front of the house. Slowly I walked back into the living room, to the middle, to a chair. I glanced at it, then I looked away. It doesn't matter, Annie. It's a chair, that's all. Pick it up. Come.

I carried it out the door, and lifted it onto the cart.

Part Three

FALL
&
WINTER

On the morning of the wedding a fine drizzle was falling, dripping off trees and buildings as slowly as it collected. We were standing outside Town Hall, under the roof of the bicycle shed: Mrs. Vos, Father, Nel, Sini, who had come home yesterday, me—and most of Winterswijk's Jews.

"That Ies de Leeuw is sure in a hurry," a passerby called out. "Had to make up for lost time, I guess," someone answered.

Father did not seem to hear. He was too busy looking down the street that led to the station. From the opposite direction two people were moving toward us. They got off their bicycles. Confused, they looked around.

"Johan and Dientje," Sini and I shouted, running up to them. They had come! We hugged. Father had seen them, too. "Magda," he said proudly, "These are the people who hid Annie and Sini. They've come by bicycle all the way from Usselo."

Briefly she looked at their faces, then, curiously, at the rest of them.

"How d'you do, Mrs. er—"

"Call her Magda," Father suggested.

"Hello," Mrs. Vos said, and turned back to the other guests.

Bong, bong, bong-bong, the bell in the church clock began to strike. Father brushed the rain off his coat, then brushed his coat over again, even though there were no more drops. He walked to the corner, to check the street leading to the station again. But Rachel must not have changed her mind. He came back, took Mrs. Vos's arm, and started to walk up the steps to Town Hall. So did Sini and I, Johan and Dientje, and the other guests. It was time.

In the Wedding Room we sat down—Sini next to me, then Nel. For a second I glanced behind me. Johan and Dientje were staring at Mrs. Vos. Their faces were blank.

The door opened again. "Isn't it wonderful? How can she do it?" people were whispering as Mrs. Menko came in, leaning on someone's arm and holding a cane. She slowly walked to her place.

A man in a black suit strode in after her, leafed through some papers, and without wasting any more time, began to speak. "I, as the registrar of this Town Hall, will marry you in accordance with the civil law of the Netherlands."

I looked out the window at the hands of the

church clock. It would take fifteen minutes, Sini
had said. Soon it would be over; but then Sini would
go back to Enschede. She had been home for one
whole day, though. Almost one day anyway, and
last night she had not gone anywhere, either. She
had sat on my bed instead, talked. She loved being
a nurse. As long as the patients weren't too sick.
I shook my head. That Sini. I moved a little closer.

"Magda Vos and Ies de Leeuw, may this day
remain an unforgettable one for both of you and
for all who are dear to you." Then solemnly and
slowly the registrar pronounced them man and
wife.

Now I looked. He was giving Father a pen, then
Mrs. Vos, and Mrs. Menko, who was a witness.
Before he picked up his papers, the registrar signed.
Father was married.

I had not gone over yet to congratulate them. I
kept hiding behind people who already had. Father
was coming toward me, I saw. To talk to me again?
No. He put his arm around my shoulder and kissed
me. "Well, Annie? Shall we go?"

Wait, wait, not so fast.

"Ies," Mrs. Vos called. "Come here."

I smiled at Father's back. Now I had time to do a
little more thinking. I had seen a great deal of her

during the last few days. She had wanted so much done, and done perfectly. I had a problem there, she said. I sighed.

Sometimes she acted strangely. As she had when I showed her the dress I was going to wear today, the one Dientje had made for me with the little checks. It made me look like a peasant, she said. Nel had thought so, too. Carefully I smoothed down the dress. And outside, before the ceremony, with Johan and Dientje. She had turned away from them. They had not liked it. They'd looked embarrassed. She must have been nervous. It was not easy for her, Father had said. I should be patient, and it would all come.

What was I going to call her though? Aunt Magda, as Sini did? Mrs. de Leeuw? No. Mother? I wiped my face. It was hot in here. I could not wait any longer. I had to speak to her. She was standing alone. That wouldn't last long. "Excuse me," I said. "What d'you want me to call you?" Tensely I waited. Would she say it herself?

"Call me whatever you want to," she answered smiling.

"Mother," I whispered.

She touched my cheek.

"Mother." I repeated it as I walked away, but to myself. I'd have to get used to it again—Mother, Mother. After all, I didn't have to say it every time

I talked to her. Mother. I turned. Was she looking at me? No. She was pretty, I had to admit that. So was her dress. "It's an old one," she had said and laughed. Still . . . it had tucks and pleats, and lace around the throat. No wonder Father had been in such a hurry.

Nel would not be living with us. She was going off to finishing school. As early as tomorrow. Far away . . . to Amsterdam, on the other side of Holland. There would only be me at home.

I took another look. She was beautiful. I could already see myself walking into town with her. "Is that her mother?" people would ask. I was lucky.

With my face burning, I joined Sini and Johan. It was still drizzling. Silently the drops were sliding off the coats of the people who were waiting in line outside Town Hall. They were there to get forms allowing them to buy hot-water bottles, pots, pans, blankets. Johan and I were waiting for Sini to go. She had to leave early, to get her ride back to Enschede.

"Good-bye," we said. "See you soon."

"It's too bad she couldn't stay longer," Johan said as he collected their bicycles. "If you ask me, nothing's gone right today."

Nothing? It had not been so bad for me! Pretty good, in fact.

"I must say, Annie, it was a shock when the

letter came. I've got to be honest. I didn't know what I was reading at first. 'Getting married?' We didn't even know your father was seeing anyone. We couldn't sleep that night from worrying about it. 'Fui-fui,' Ma kept saying, 'that little Annie.' She wanted me to go and see the woman right away. 'We've got to make sure she's right for her,' she said." He shook his head. "How could I have done that, Annie? It was already too late. We only got the letter a few days ago. The mail still doesn't get delivered right."

"Johan." Excitedly Dientje was coming down the steps. "I just had a nice talk with Ies. He took me into a corner and said, 'Dientje, what d'you think of my wife.' Ja, he wanted me to tell him. It made a difference to'm to know, I think." Quickly she added, "She's a good-looking woman, Johan. That, I had to say."

"Good-looking, good-looking." Johan sounded angry. "She'd better be good to Annie. That's what matters, Dientje. Nothing else. I wish Ies would've asked me. That's what I would have told him."

"You sometimes make mistakes, too, Johan. When Ies came to see us that time, you never opened your mouth. If you had, we would be a lot happier now."

"What do you mean?" Johan asked.

"You know," Dientje said, looking at me, her face getting red. "But it wouldn't be right to say—not today."

"All right, woman, all right. We didn't come to ruin Annie's day. We're making her all upset. Come, Dientje, here." He handed her the bicycle. "How's the knee?"

"It doesn't matter, Johan."

"Damn. If only the buses were running. . . . Well, we're going to the house anyway. You can take it easy there. We'll keep Annie company, talk with her, for a couple of hours. We haven't seen her for over a month. We've got things to say. Eh, Dientje?"

She began to smile a little.

I let out my breath. Maybe we should go right now, not wait here another minute. Except for Mrs. Menko, who had already gone home, everyone else was getting organized to come back with us. "Wait for me, Bernard." "Put up your collar, Bettie."

"Come, Johan and Dientje," I urged. We wouldn't want to miss any of the party, either.

All the way back from Town Hall, Father kept turning around. He was still looking for Rachel.

· 2 ·

Another cart and another farmer had brought it all, Mrs. Vos's furniture, in many trips. "You're really making our road look beautiful, Ies," Maria had said, holding her goat back and watching as one piece after another had been carried inside: the sofa and chairs with carvings of fruit and flowers on the arms, the mahogany sideboard, the china cabinet, the rug, with flowers, too.

Dientje did not have to tiptoe in our house. You could not hear footsteps anyway. Here, I'd prove it to her. Firmly I led her across the rug, arm in arm.

"It's something, Annie, this rug. For the feet yet. It's so fancy."

That's what the guests were saying about the dinner table. They were all crowded around it. "It's spectacular, Magda." There was awe in their voices. "How did you manage a whole platter of cookies?" "And all those eggs." "They're stuffed." "Look, look, with—What are those brown flecks in them?" " 'Sardines,' she just said." "Sardines? I don't remember what they taste like." "And bowls of salt and mustard the likes of which I haven't seen for years. Magda, how did you do it?"

"You have to know the right people, that's all," she said and laughed. "Annie, get the glasses."

Gently she pushed me toward the kitchen. "Hurry," she said. "And don't break them, they're delicate. Better make several trips."

Break them? Of course not. Did she notice how carefully I was bringing them in? They weren't trembling or sliding around the tray even a little bit. Father looked proud, I saw. He probably had not thought I could do it. It was nice to come into the living room and hear cheerful voices. It was really a party! I had never been to anything like this before. I liked it. "Excuse me," I warned a man who was taking a step back. Holding my breath, I lowered the tray to the table. There, the glasses were in place, and all in one piece.

Mother went to the closet and opened it wide. She pulled out a dark green bottle and began to pour small quantities of red wine into each glass.

"Magda, how is this possible?" everyone asked. "There isn't any in the stores yet."

"I hid it with my furniture," she explained, "so it's really aged, you might say. But it was already a fine bottle—1929, an excellent year. My first husband knew all about wines. Remember the wedding?" she asked. "How elegant we all looked then! You, Bettie, wore a long pink gown with ruffles, and satin shoes."

Thinking about it made Bettie smile.

"And you, Bernard, a real matching suit." Sheepishly Bernard grinned at his blue pants and brown jacket.

"If you ask me," Johan said, looking around the table, "I'm the only one here who's dressed right. I've got my wedding suit on."

"This is not Usselo," Mother informed him. "Remember," she said in a softer voice, "how many guests there were? Almost every Jew in Winterswijk came to the wedding—close to three hundred. I count twenty now."

"Please, Magda, don't talk about that," Father said.

Silently they all raised their glasses. "To all of us here," Father said solemnly, "but especially to Johan and Dientje Oosterveld. If it had not been for people like them, none of us would be here now."

Lovingly Johan looked at me. "It was worth all the danger, Ies," he said. "And there was a lot, believe me. But I've never had wine before as far as that goes." He tilted his head back and finished it. "Awfully sour, Dientje, watch it. But wait a minute, how old did you say this was, Magda. 1929? No wonder! It's gone stale, I bet." Gratefully everyone looked at Johan as they began to laugh. He joined in, looking puzzled though.

"It's called dry, Johan," Mother snapped.

"What was that, Magda? Dry?" He wiped a

drop off his chin and showed it to her. "I always say you have to get up a lot earlier to kid a farmer than to kid anyone else." He laughed again, not looking puzzled any longer.

People began to mill around, their wineglasses in their hands. "You come, too, Dientje," Johan said, no glass in his.

She did not want to. Gingerly she touched a few of the things on the table, the cloth, a vase. "I've got to try everything, Annie, so I can tell the others in Usselo about it. I bet they've never been to a place like this." With the utmost care her finger moved on to something else.

"I think you're impressed, Dientje," Mother said when she passed by. She laughed. "You should be. Everything was expensive enough."

Dientje did not hear her.

"We've got more important things to do, Annie," Johan said. "You and me, right? We're going to sit someplace. Come, these chairs look like nice soft ones. Ah—" He bent down and looked at his legs. "No wonder Magda didn't like the suit. I've still got the bicycle clip on. There, that's better."

"Yes, Johan." Much. He was not even wearing his thick black socks and *klompen* today.

"Ja, I'm fancy," Johan said, looking at his shoes,

too. "You never saw them on me, I guess, because Dientje and I didn't go anywhere when you lived with us. They've gotten smaller, I think." He loosened his shoelaces. "There," he sighed, leaning back. "Now tell me what you'll be learning in school."

I didn't yet know exactly, but I said, "Languages, math, physics."

"Physics?" Johan repeated. "What are those?"

I didn't yet know that either, but it had something to do with formulas.

"Formulas?" Delighted, Johan slapped his leg. "That's what I give the calves. Don't tell me I've been doing physics all my life, and no one ever even taught me. I'm not surprised though. I was good in school, Annie, especially at subtracting. 'Does Johan Oosterveld know the answer?' the teacher always asked. I'm not kidding. Every time something difficult came up. While the other kids were still figuring things out on paper, I already knew it. I loved school, Annie. Couldn't wait to put my good pants on in the morning and run down the road. Well, here we are."

He sighed. He looked over at Dientje. She was still standing by the table. "I think I can say what I want to say without her, Annie." Quickly he began. "We want you to be happy, Ma, Dientje, and me. Don't forget. But if things don't work out

—they will, don't worry—but if they don't, you come to us. Because that's what our house is. Home for you. Always. You hear?"

"I know, Johan." Beautiful, this room. The pinks and browns and greens, the flowers—everything. And Johan and Dientje were here.

Near us Father and his friends were discussing leather goods and woolens. Business was getting better, but slowly apparently. "That Max, he was shrewd, beginning again in scrap metal. You know how much of that's around."

"No wonder he had to leave; he doesn't have the time."

"Before we know it, Ies, he'll be shipping old iron to America and bringing back brand-new cars."

"I wish that man could ship me a tractor, Annie. Wouldn't that be something? What I could do with one of those!" Johan said.

"Annie." From the back of the room came Mother's voice.

I got up. "I'll be back as soon as I can, Johan," I promised.

Absentmindedly he nodded. I took a few steps, then looked back. Johan was beaming. Maybe he was imagining himself already sitting on a tractor. He saw me, and waved. "Don't take long, Annie. Eh?"

I shook my head. "Don't worry, Johan."

Did Mother know I was there? She kept on talking. "It wasn't easy to get Nel into that school, let me tell you. They don't take just anyone. Difficult courses they give. Household management is one of them. . . ."

Bettie nodded enviously. "I hope she learns to run a household better than I do, Magda."

"Embroidery, intermediate French, plus fancy cooking as soon as the ingredients are available. Right, Nel?" Now Mother knew I was there. "I'll be needing you soon, Annie. Nel, tell Bettie about your roommate. . . ."

I hurried back to Johan. His face had changed, I saw. He wasn't beaming any more. He must be thinking about the money a tractor would cost. "C'mon, Annie," he said, looking up. He patted the empty chair next to him. "I was wondering where you were."

Father's group had gone on to talk of something else, I heard—silks.

"In a way I hate to be here today," Johan said, after I had sat down. "But I'm glad to have a chance to see you again. That's what really matters to me, Annie. Who knows when it'll happen again? Eighty kilometers a day on the bike is a lot in the kind of weather we'll be getting. And the bus station in Enschede doesn't know a thing yet. I had Sini ask. We live in the wrong part of Holland, they said. If it was Amsterdam, it wouldn't be a problem; there'd be a bus." Frustrated he looked at me. "I can't win."

Silently we watched Dientje move away from the table. She saw us and came over. Smiling apologetically, she sat down.

"It was getting about time, woman," Johan said. "Hanging around all that stuff. She won't like what we've got at home any more, Annie." He laughed. "She'll want to buy things, too, eh?"

Dientje winked at me.

"Annie." Mother beckoned. "Come."

"What are you jumping up for now," Johan complained. "We just got settled."

Yes, yes, I know. But Mother needed me.

"Don't take so long this time," Johan said.

It was though—taking long. Every time I passed Johan and Dientje, they asked, "Aren't you done yet?"

No. So many things had to be taken care of. Salt, eggs, mustard, napkins, and plates, of course. It was nice, passing things around. Everyone looked happy when they saw me. "Thank you, Annie," they said. "You're wonderful."

Of course I wasn't, but it made me smile anyway, hearing that. It would have been even nicer if Mother had said so. But it was too soon for that, I knew. I had to have more patience.

And on I went, carrying the tray the right way —out and a little up—exactly as Mother had shown me. "Thank you, Annie," people said, "thank you."

What did Johan want now? I shook my head. No, I was still not through.

"Come here a minute anyway, Annie. Isn't Nel going to help you?"

"I'm not sure."

"Annie looks awfully tired, Johan. She can't do it all by herself."

"I know, woman. Why d'you think I asked?"

Well? Was that all? Impatiently I walked away. I wished Johan had not said what he had about Nel though. I glanced over at her. Talking with Mother . . . still.

I went to the table for another set of plates, with flowers, too, around the borders. And on to the next person, tray just right. "Have some, Mrs. van Gelder?" But it was not the same now. Johan had spoiled it.

"Johan." I touched him on the shoulder.

He looked up. "Are you through?"

Firmly I nodded. Yes.

"Well then." He laughed. "We can talk about a lot of things. Eh? Here I've been so busy sitting I've forgotten to give you Opoe's regards. She's fine. She's wondering when she can see you. You should hear her, Annie, when Sini comes. 'That could be our Sini,' and laughing! She would have come today just to see you if there'd been a bus. And you know Opoe; she doesn't leave the house easily. Last wedding she was at was ours, Dientje."

"Ah, that was not the same."

"It was raining then, too, woman, worse than this. But it didn't matter, Dientje, did it? The house looked beautiful, even from the outside. Remember the greens over the kitchen door?" Grimacing a little, he swallowed the rest of the egg he was eating. "Bah," he said, "sardines and eggs don't go together." Quickly he went on. "Remember the cow your mother gave us, Dientje? Ha, ha, I got it out of her, didn't I? That cow was a beauty, Annie. You should have seen her coming down the road with the neighbors. A string of flowers around the horns, a mirror in between them, and they were all singing. You could hear it all over Usselo. 'Fui-fui,' Opoe kept saying when we got to the house, 'just for a wedding. No, that I can't see.' Those crazy neighbors stopped off first at the baker's, and before he knew what he had on his hands, she had helped herself to a loaf of whole wheat. 'That's the cow for Johan,' everyone hollered. 'She's got plenty of spunk.' "

"Not so loud, Johan." Anxiously Dientje poked him in the side.

"Leave me alone. I didn't ride this far to whisper. They put us on a chair, woman, remember?"

"Paper flowers around the back of it, Johan—"

"And they lifted us. High and low, and high and low, we went."

"I had to pull my skirt down, hold it to the chair; it was that wild." Dientje giggled.

Me, too. Just as I had the first time, I heard Johan tell the story.

"And while we were doing the waltz to the accordion and singing, 'Had I but never wed, would not have any regret,'—but it was already too late—everyone was twirling paper ribbons around us. After a while, I had trouble moving the feet."

"I was scared, Johan, I had 'em twirled around the throat—"

"Ah, you always scream for nothing. And the food we had! Remember, Dientje? Plenty of beer and a juicy piece of pork?"

"And beef, Johan."

"You're damned right. Two kinds of meat, pota-toes, green beans, and a dish of chocolate pudding at the end."

Dientje defended Mother. "But Magda couldn't do that. Don't forget, Johan, you still can't get everything."

"It's time to come back, Annie," Mother called. She sounded impatient.

I followed Johan's eyes to the table, to the plat-ter with cookies, the coffee cups, saucers, sugar, milk, spoons. Slowly I got up and looked for the tray. With both hands I carried it away, but only a little up.

The guests had left, all of them, Johan and Dientje last. They had stood in the doorway for a long time, silent, their collars up. The bicycle path would be muddy, and slippery with leaves that had been coming down for days. The leaves would wind themselves around the tires—splash—get stuck, fall off. . . . Slowly the rear lights of their bicycles were moving away. Opoe would still be up when they got home. She'd rush to the door, ask.

I hadn't had a good time at the party, either. I had not liked seeing them sit there, arms folded, waiting. I sighed. Things would be easier tomor-row. No Nel. No Johan and Dientje.

Two dots, the bicycle lights, tiny ones. Barely specks now. Then darkness.

· 3 ·

All over town, doors were opening, letting in the morning air, which was fresh and a little chilly. They closed again, behind people going to work and to shop, and behind hundreds of children, going to school. Rapidly I walked down the road. They'd be waiting, the kids, wouldn't they? Had they forgotten? It had been a while since I had seen Jannie. I should have asked her exactly where—

I smiled. There she was, in front of her house, with another girl—Selma—but she did not look as nice. "Hi," I said to both of them.

Well, aren't we going to leave? What if we're late? "Jannie?"

"Not yet," she said laughing. We had to wait for the others.

I blushed. I had forgotten all about them. Worried, I looked at the other houses. C'mon, c'mon, we don't have all day. There, three doors had opened, and out they came, kids with clean, pressed clothes. The boy Kees's hair was so neat that the comb marks still showed.

"Now," Jannie said, and off we went.

And talking! They couldn't stop. "Hope the teachers are nice." "Hope they don't make us work too hard." For whatever they hoped, Jannie had an answer, a good one. "Can't wait, can't wait," everyone yelled.

Can't wait? I stopped. Was there something in my shoe? I took it off, held it upside down. No. So many new kids. They wouldn't stare at me, would they? Say anything, about my legs? And I'd know as much as the others, wouldn't I, not seem stupid? Sure, Sini had taught me things, especially math— but she had not always understood it herself. And never geography or history or—there must be other things. It had been so long since I'd gone to school—fourth grade. What if I had forgotten what to do? I'd watch the others. They would know. Where were they? Quickly I slipped my foot back into the shoe and ran after them.

"The principal," the kids around me whispered.

"Come with me," he said, but nicely. He took me to my classroom. The teachers knew how much school I had missed, he said. "Don't worry about it. You'll catch up. Even if you don't do well for a while, don't worry." He mussed my hair. He was sure it would come, he said. "There, sit in the front."

Quickly I nodded. Yes, that would be better. Stealthily I turned around. Too bad Jannie was in another grade, a higher one. But Selma was in my class; she sat right behind me.

So many teachers, and all in one day. I yawned, and slouched just a little bit. That would be all right? For a minute? Wearily I watched another teacher walk to the front of the room. He picked up a piece of chalk, wrote his name on the blackboard, and began to talk. I shot up in my chair. This one was speaking German. *"Guten Mittag."*

It's a teacher speaking, Annie. Look at him. It's not a soldier in the street, not Hitler on the radio. You don't have to be afraid. No boots, no uniform. A suit.

"Ich bin . . . du bist . . ."

No. Tomorrow I'd listen to this teacher, not today. I would write to Johan and Dientje tonight, a nice letter telling them not to worry. Mother and I were getting along so well. We had a talk yesterday, almost the minute she came back from the station. And I had been afraid she wouldn't even want to see me she had been so upset when she went to see Nel off. Of course she was still sad, just as I had been after Sini left, and Rachel. Maybe she'd like to sit down. "Here, Mother." Then I did, too. Close, but just a little.

"I feel lost with Nel gone, Annie. We have been together a long time, even in hiding. It seems unbelievable that suddenly she's not here any more."

Solemnly I nodded. Yes. But she'd get over it. I'd better not say that though.

"What I haven't gone through! I often think how is it possible for one person to have suffered so much. Here I am in a strange house with people I hardly know. With Nel around, I didn't mind. But without her. . . ."

I stared out the window. Maybe we could do something special today. Not a celebration—of course not. But something. What? Startled I looked back at Mother. Had that to do with her suffering, too? What she had just said? That I had come to her knowing practically nothing? It must have. She looked so serious. "I even said to your father, 'So many people took care of her and not one of them bothered to teach her anything. The result is that I have a lot of hard work ahead of me.' You don't even know how to make a bed properly."

No? Dientje had always admired the way I did it. "What that Annie can't do with a bed," she used to say.

"You even have trouble drawing open the drapes, so they hang right."

I checked. Stuck behind the chair again. But that could be fixed. There, already done, and I hadn't been gone for more than a second.

"Dust . . . do dishes. Your table manners, Annie,

badly need to be improved. Please, watch me from now on. As to your appearance—"Mother sighed. "I honestly don't know where to begin."

I studied my hands. The tips of my fingers were still wrinkled from having washed the wedding dishes.

"All right, I'll begin at the top. Your hair. It's always messy. Pull it to the side for a minute, and let me see something. I was afraid of that. From now on, include your ears when you wash." Her eyes moved down. "Of course, there's your clothes—but I can't do much about them yet. Manners and appearance are important, Annie, even though at this moment you may think they're not. They tell what kind of a person you really are, and that's not a peasant." Mother looked around the living room, stroking the arm of her chair. "We now have a position in this town."

I puckered my forehead. Father had bought three cows last week, and he'd been very happy about it. Is that what she meant? Confused, I looked at her.

"You're still young enough to learn," Mother went on, "which is lucky. Another year and I might have come too late. The best thing now is for you to forget the old and get right into the new. I hope you can do it, Annie. I get upset easily.

That's not good for me. Nel was always wonderful about that. She never gave me trouble."

I wouldn't, either. She didn't have to be afraid. I just hoped I could remember it all. There was so much—everything, as she said.

I moved a little closer to her, but our talk must be over. Mother was getting up. Maybe I could do something for her, do it perfectly, show her I could learn fast. She gave me her coat to hang up. It had an especially big collar, a fur one, with a face, eyes, mouth, teeth. Carefully I held the coat away from me as I carried it into the hall. I hung it on the first peg. . . .

"*Annie.*"

Frightened, I looked at the teacher.

"I'm glad someone is interested in this class. You didn't even hear the bell. You're a good girl. Go home."

I got up. "Thank you," I said politely. It had been nice, yesterday, sitting with Mother for so long, doing nothing, like a lady. I was going to write Sini and Rachel tonight, tell them not to worry either. But first . . . There were all those words I had gotten right today on the spelling test —more than half. "*Hij bloedt*" had been one of them. I had not forgotten to put in the "d," even though the teacher had tried to trick us by accenting the "t" as he said it. But I wouldn't boast to Mother, just mention it as if it were nothing special. . . .

She was writing a letter as I hurried in. "Not now, Annie," she said. "If I can finish this quickly, Nel will have it before the end of the week."

Sure. I sat down, waited, checked the clock. Such a long letter it was turning out to be. There, she'd sealed the envelope. "Mother—"

Even her handwriting is beautiful, I thought, as I ran to the post office. Those spelling words? What of them? They had been easy, and I had gotten only half of them right anyway.

· 4 ·

At the end of October we received a letter from Rachel; not from the town she had gone to, from another one—Renkum—where the big sanatorium was.

"Dear Father, I won't be getting the teaching job I wrote you about after all. Something has happened. I had to have a physical, the last barrier, I'd hoped, before they hired me. It was a long examination; 'no doubt because the doctor's new in town,' my 'family' said when I came home. The old one wasn't so fussy. This one took X rays, too.

"When I went back a few days later for the results, I was told"—Father stopped for a moment, then he read on, bending his head—"that I have tuberculosis. How did I get it? I asked the doctor. He's not sure. But there has to be something in town that causes it, he said. People in other places have been undernourished and crowded together in small rooms. They don't have tuberculosis. He has found it in three other applicants for the job. He suspects it's the canal. Father, how could I have known that? I've been sitting there every night since I came back here. Sure, I saw people dump scrub water into it, and fill up their teakettles. It seemed dirty to me. But more—no. Maybe I should've known it was dangerous when I saw the fish come up for air. But I grabbed them, too, just like the others. No standing in line and no coupons, we all thought as we carried them home. I don't know why that upsets me so now. I ate them during the war. Who knows what else is in that canal? Spit, and what not. I've done a lot of thinking since I arrived here. Working in that store didn't help me either, I now see. . . . ."

"I saw that the minute she wrote about it, Ies. *Brr*. Used American clothes, who knows who's been in them?"

Father went on. "When a new shipment came in, and the people rushed over, all breathing in my face —everyone was always looking for black. I never wrote you that, I guess. They wanted to be properly dressed again in case of another funeral. I see what I've just said. Don't worry, Father, I'll be fine. And I didn't get sick in the past two months either. I've had it for a long time, the doctor said. That's why it'll take a while to get better. Fortunately I'm used to waiting."

When Father finished reading us the letter, he went to the telephone to call Rachel. In a few seconds he was back. He couldn't talk to her. She was not allowed out of bed.

"How long will she have to be there?" I asked. Rachel had not really said.

Father took off his glasses. "A year or two, they think."

"Well, that's life," Mother said.

"Why did she have to be hidden in that town?" he asked. His voice shook.

That, Mother did not know. "First she becomes religious there," she said, "and now this."

Father left, quietly closing the door behind him. The letter was still on the table, open.

"P.S.," I read. "Please take Annie to a doctor. She's so frail. What if I gave it to her?"

I could have it, too? Mother must also have read that part. She was already running to the telephone.

· 5 ·

Just a few weeks later, judges from England, France, Russia, and the United States traveled to a city in Germany called Nuremberg. Twenty-one of Hitler's closest friends and helpers were waiting there to be tried for having planned and started the war. Rachel's war, Father's, Mother's, Sini's, Johan and Dientje's, so many other people's. Practically the whole world's. Mine.

It was the same city people had traveled to for nine hundred years, to look at the houses and churches, to eat in the inns, walk along the winding streets, sketchbooks in their hands. The same city, too, where in the thirties and early forties they had gotten together, those twenty-one, for their party's annual meeting. Again many people came—tens of thousands at once this time. Just for that. And for Hitler's speech. "Heil!" they screamed, with their right hands raised in the Nazi salute. And their eyes full of hate. Toward Jews, Slavs, gypsies, Communists, priests, and Germans who weren't any of those, who just thought differently. "Heil!" Nazi voices had roared in the September sun. "We are with you, Hitler. You know what's right. You know what we need. Heil! Heil! Heil!"

It was not the same Nuremberg any more, the papers said. The churches and inns were gone, and piles of rubble covered the little winding streets. Allied bombs. . . . But the jail was still standing, and so was the courthouse, untouched.

When the trial opened, the accused men were fidgety, bored. They hardly listened to the prosecutor as he recounted their crimes. One of Hitler's friends fell asleep. That bored. But he woke up in time to grab the microphone and say what the other twenty had already said, "*Nein.*" Not guilty —of anything.

"Not guilty?" most people in Holland shouted. "What's the matter with them?"

Don't worry, the papers answered. The proof is there, in Nuremberg. Those men had carefully written everything down, all their plans, and forgotten to destroy the documents when the war ended.

When they were shown a movie of what had taken place in their camps, they covered their eyes, couldn't watch.

At least the men are no longer bored, the papers announced.

"No longer bored!" the people of Holland

shouted. "Hang them. They don't even deserve a
trial. A lot of talking and what for?"

Not everyone shouted. Some cried—those who
had lost relatives and friends in the camps and read
what had happened to them every day when the
newspaper came. I would have liked to go over to
Mother and comfort her. I was afraid to, even
though the doctor had said I did not have tuberculosis. What if Mother was right and the incubation
period could be longer for some people?

November went on. With school, going either
alone or with Jannie and the others; the masseur
afterward; coming back home fast, always. That's
what Mother liked. "How come you're late,
Annie?" she'd say at the door, even though I never
was. Nice.

I didn't mind too much, about Nel. The stories
Mother told, the letters she read, the telephone calls
she discussed. I hardly mentioned my sisters any
more, or Johan or Dientje. Mother did not seem
interested in hearing about them; she always interrupted when I began: "That has to do with the old,
Annie."

I sighed.

"Did you hear what I just said, Annie?"

"Where did Nel go now, Mother?"

"She went to two parties over the weekend.

Now you can see how important it is for people to look good. Appearances make all the difference in the world."

I smiled. I was working on that. My ears hurt from all the scrubbing. No, I didn't mind about Nel, not much. Only sometimes. But then I'd forget, the minute Mother said, "And now, Annie, ..." Anything could come. Not necessarily Nel!

More traveling was done at the beginning of that winter. The deadline in Walcheren had been met, except for one hole. Special buses went around Holland, to pick up the last of the island's refugees.

A bus came to Winterswijk, too. It stopped in the marketplace. "Do you have any cats to give me?" the driver asked. "Good, all of you are carrying boxes, I see. Hand them to me, and I'll put them on the back seats." That's what the people of Walcheren had asked for, since the island cats had drowned a long time ago when the water first came, and there were many rats now.

Knives, too, the refugees took home, sturdy ones, to scrape off the mussels that the North Sea had deposited on their floors and walls. They said good-bye. "Hope we did not stay too long, and that it wasn't too much for you."

"Think nothing of it," their Winterswijk hosts assured them. "We did it with pleasure."

"Come and see us," the islanders shouted from the bus. The ornaments on the old-fashioned lace caps trembled as the women moved their heads. "But give us a while to clean the place up first, get the salt out of the soil, plant some things. Then you come."

I would; I would. Mother had never been there, either. We could all go, when the island looked pretty again, as it had in the picture book I had once seen. "Good-bye."

And Sini, she traveled, too. She might even be on the train right now while I was walking away from the marketplace. She had a new job, taking care of small children whose parents couldn't. What had Mother said about that after dinner? I laughed. For someone not interested in my "old people," she certainly spent enough time talking about them. Every time a letter came. Last night had been Sini's turn.

"She's a very flighty girl. Anyone can see that. She's no Nel. And mark my words, she won't last more than a month at this job, either. She doesn't have what it takes." Mother had stopped filing her nails and looked over at Father. He was sitting near the stove, his legs stuck out, once in a while contentedly wriggling his toes in the direction of the flames that shone red and blue behind the mica door.

"I shouldn't have gone to the library for him,"

Mother complained. "Once you give that man a book he's lost. My first husband was also a cattle dealer, but not like this. He loved to dance, tell jokes. He made me laugh. I'm not used to all this reading. What does your father see in it night after night?"

He'd stop soon; he did not have that many more pages to go.

"I hate to think of the next few months," Mother continued, "sitting here by myself. Nel was right—this might just as well be Siberia for all the people I see out here. And evenings will get a lot longer before they get shorter."

I knew. They were long. Especially now that I no longer had time to read. Father's toes again, wriggling. Would Mother like me to teach her some English? That would make a big difference, she'd see. She could listen to the songs on the radio, know what they were about. And I was good at English. "Would you like me to, Mother?"

A pity. Mother didn't think she needed any. It would have been nice. "Go fix the drapes, Annie. You still don't draw them right. I sometimes wonder whether you ever will."

It was my own fault that Mother was annoyed. I should not have told her I was good at English. Maybe Nel was doing badly in school, and Mother was worried. But I was not good at everything—not at math or physics or gym. I was very bad at gym. "I have trouble jumping across the rope unless it is practically lying on the floor." That had been the right thing to say. She was smiling again.

After a while, Father closed his book. "Come, Magda, let's go for a walk," he said. "I've been sitting all evening."

That made Mother laugh. "Now? At this hour? We'll break our necks." But she went anyway, with him and the flashlight as usual. After the book. And our talks before that. Father—all dressed up these days. "A new wife, new rules, Annie," he said every morning, happily as he went to work, a tie sticking up from his old vest. . . .

I stopped walking, squinted. Was that Mother standing in front of the house? Yes. Quickly I patted my hair down.

"Come here, Annie," she beckoned.

Yes, yes. How wonderful that she had come all the way to the road. And I had stopped in the marketplace for only ten minutes.

The letter to Nel had been mailed, the potatoes peeled, the vegetables washed, my homework done. It was almost dark.

Quietly I was setting the table, making sure

everything was in the right place. Father had come home. I'd heard the back door. He wouldn't come all the way in yet, not until he'd taken his shoes and jacket off and brushed his pants. Then "Here I am, wife," he'd say, "and I think not even you can tell that I have been with the cows all day."

There, just as I thought. He must be giving her a kiss now. She'd smile, fix his tie, ask him whether he had had a good day.

"Guess how much I got for that skinny cow this morning, the one I kept in the meadow across the road," he'd say.

"It was worth at least four hundred guilders, Ies. If you let it go for less, you're a fool."

"That's exactly how much I got for it, Magda," he exclaimed. "Four hundred."

"I told you it was worth that much," she said laughing. "Didn't I? I haven't been wrong yet, Ies."

"No, you haven't." Father would rub his hands and comment on the cooking smells. "Even they're a miracle, Magda."

They'd be in any minute now. I made a last check of the table. Yes, yes, no—a nasty spot on the serving spoon. Quick, polish it on my dress. I'd like meals if I could serve myself, but I never took enough food, Mother said, when she had let me.

My clothes had begun to pinch though, and it wasn't my imagination as Mother kept telling me. I had red lines across my stomach when I took off my skirt at night.

The kitchen door opened. Dinner did smell good. She was a wonderful cook. Only I wish she'd listen to me when I said, "No more, please."

Carefully I put the serving spoon back on the table, handle toward Mother's plate.

· 6 ·

Christmas vacations everywhere were going to be very short this year. We had already missed so much school that we shouldn't have any vacation at all, the principal stated. That made everyone laugh, a little suspiciously though. What if he meant it?

He didn't. "Enjoy your few days," he said. That really made us laugh.

Well, then, I could do a lot, make plans as some of the kids already were under their breath. I could ask someone to my house. Yes, that would be nice. I thought about it for a minute. Jannie? She was too old. But there was Selma. I could learn to like her. After all, we were in the same class. She might even be very pleased to get away from the boys. They were always teasing her, especially Kees. Even when there was hardly any snow, he'd wear himself out collecting some in his bare hands, just to put it down her back. She never knew what to do. Shrieking, waving her arms, didn't stop him. I glanced out the window for a second. There was already enough snow on the ground for her to be buried in. She'd be happy to come to my house.

Early in the afternoon maybe, on the first day of vacation, she'd come. We'd make a snowman in our garden—a big round one, with arms. And I'd ask Mother to let us have things to dress him in. We'd have a little tea afterward, to warm up. Maybe Mother would make it, call us when it was ready. "Annie, come and bring your friend." Yes. And offer us a cookie—homemade. Selma would love that, she'd probably want to come again a few days later. Another snowman? I'd see.

"Selma," the teacher warned. "If you don't stop fooling around, we'll have to open the school just for you."

Worried, I looked behind me. She was hurriedly nodding yes to a couple of kids, I saw. Had they already asked? So soon? It was not even three o'clock yet. Quickly I turned back. I must already be too late. It was all right though. I hardly knew her. I'd wait a little longer, till spring. I'd still have a good time. Nel was not coming home, and Mother had not even been sad. She smiled instead, and said Nel would definitely have made the long trip to our house and given up her parties if Mother had asked. But she had not wanted to. Contentedly I stared at the pencil jar.

"Let us stop for a minute," churches all over Holland urged people, "and reflect. Last year, our cupboards were bare, our stores empty. Potato soup and a crust of bread were all we had. Whereas now there is an abundance again. Yet, some among us are, for whatever reason, still lacking. Let us be generous to them. Let us give; follow the example of the Americans who, more than any other nation, have shared with us. Go. Go. And let the light and joy of Christmas be with you."

As the people came out, organ music did, too, solemnly following them as they strode past the stores where the windows were still covered with boards. But the pieces of glass in the middle were glowing—wherever a streetlamp was near. On this Sunday they were already lit, although it was not completely dark. Leather belts in De Wind's Mode encircled a handbag. Next to them was a cotton dress, a winter coat, and the notice that still read,

"For Display." But they were smiling at the sign today, the people, as they stopped to look again, some of the men in real matching suits that had come all the way from America. New ones. Yes, too big, but not for much longer. "Not with all the food we'll be getting." Smiling happily.

The next day, the calm was gone. Early, early, into the streets, coupons in hands, bags on arms. Recklessly people turned corners—but politely. "Pardon me." "Excuse me." "Didn't mean to." So many special things to be bought, and the day was short.

One orange, one ounce of chocolate but six different shapes to choose from, two whole ounces of tobacco, one extra scoop of sugar, one bag of flour, one piece of chicken, and for every family, one jar of brown powder, which didn't look like coffee but "was the new thing in America," the grocer assured suspicious shoppers. Twice as many potatoes, a pound of red beets, scouring powder for afterward.

"I told you people months ago, didn't I," Maria shouted, running, too, without her goat. "Radios don't lie."

"Look 'ere, look 'ere. Buy one. Brighten up your door." The people ran back to the marketplace. "Sure we want a wreath. So much, so much. Almost takes two to carry it all home."

And the bakers—they gave space in their ovens to people who had none. "Bring us the ingredients. We will do your baking."

They did even more. Each baker got on his bicycle to deliver a loaf of bread to Mrs. Menko. They knew her biggest wish was to have extra, so she wouldn't run out of food. "Don't worry about coupons either, Mrs. Menko. Just get well completely."

And although we were Jewish and did not celebrate Christmas, we still shared. I went to her house, with a present, walking carefully all the way. "Don't take your eyes off the box once," Mother had warned. That I had done . . . the traffic. But it was all right. I checked every now and then, peeking under the lid. Still in the middle, the cake—almost. Wait. I wiped my thumb and nudged the slice back to where it had come from —not a dent, not even a crumb. Dientje should see. Then deftly I shifted the box to one hand, and knocked on Mrs. Menko's door.

"Everyone is taking such good care of me," she cried when she saw me. "Thank you, Annie. You're wonderful."

I wished Mother would say so. It would come; it

had to. I had hardly any of my old habits left, the "Johan-and-Dientje" ones as Mother called them. "They'll do for caves, Annie, not for houses."

Johan and Dientje . . . they wouldn't recognize me. That neat. I'd better get going. Mother, she'd want me.

"Have a good day, Mrs. Menko," I said. She looked so happy. Even with the tears. Softly I closed the door. On now, home. Empty, that box. There, under the arm with it. Not carefully either, not any longer. Plenty of time to carry it just so. When I came closer. . . .

· 7 ·

From the moment I got up on New Year's Day, the sky was gray, the air misty, dense. It stayed that way, through breakfast, lunch, dinner, afterward, and was that way now. I couldn't see anything in my room. The clock downstairs chimed, eleven times. Otherwise, no sound. Father and Mother must be asleep.

I closed my eyes. Was that singing outside? I jumped out of bed, opened the window. Men's voices, faint. Coming closer. . . . It was the song of Winterswijk's soccer team: "Hand in hand we go, friends,/For our team can't be beat./Words won't do, scoring we want/And that is—" Without waiting for the song to end, someone began all over again: "Hand in hand—" Another voice tried to stop him. "Ten Riet, not yet. We've got to stick together."

I leaned farther out. Six yellow beams of light were zigzagging on the road, lighting up wooden shoes. Six pairs, clump-clumping close together. Dark shapes on top of them, zigzagging a little, too, while they finished the song, "What we ge-e-e-e-e-e-t."

"I'd better stop singing, fellows. The wife doesn't like it any more when I'm noisy. Reminds her too much of the son. I don't want'r hearing me."

"Ah, Droppers." Ten Riet's voice was comforting. "Tonight the wife won't mind. It's New Year's, and the first time in ages we've been able to celebrate. What d'you care anyway. Who's she, I say. Eh? Here we go all of us, "Hand in—"

"Ten Riet." Mulder's voice interrupted him again. "You're not the head of the group now. I am. We just voted, remember, when we were in the café. It was unanimous."

"But next January—"

"So, Ten Riet." Mulder interrupted. "I'm the

one who tells you when to begin, when I say 'Now.' But don't make it too loud. We're almost in front of Mrs. de Leeuw's house."

"Wait a shecond." The Geerdes father must have a full pipe in his mouth. "I don't have my dzjacket on right. My arm znot in it, I don't think. Ow, Ten Riet, I pricked myshelf on your neck. What've you got on."

"Beats me," Ten Riet said. "Ja, ja . . . ja, ja, ja, ja, I feel it now."

I laughed softly.

Five flashlights shone on him. "It's a Christmas wreath, Ten Riet. You must've fallen against the café door. When we came out, maybe. And all you had was the one drink! What're we going to do with you when we can get more? You tripped over your *klompen*, too."

"Pa, when they're making 'em again," a Geerdes son said longingly, "we're going to get some. I got such holes in mine."

"How about chairs," Mulder yelled, "so you can give'm a break once in a while. Stop it, Geerdes, you're bumping into me again."

"Get wives, I say," Ten Riet shouted. "How old are the boys? Forty-nine and fifty? Eh? Eh? Eh? Sure. They're the right age."

"Where would they sit?" Mulder bellowed.

"Wives these days don't want to stand on their feet all the time."

"They could do what Ies did. Have her bring'r own."

"They shay it'sh different inshide, not as when we shaw it."

"She may even have something under the cork."

"Let's wish'm a Happy New Year." "Dammit, who's she? I say." "Let'sh ring the bell."

They shouldn't, they shouldn't. Mother wouldn't understand their fun. Wooden shoes rattling toward the front door. . . . Good. I laughed again. Mulder was calling them back.

"I wasn't the one telling you to go. As your new chairman *I* say when. Not this year, we're not going. We wait until the next."

There was Droppers' voice, for the first time in a long while. "But I'm not coming, not to that Jew's house."

"We know, Droppers, we know. C'mon, don't cry, not tonight."

They were leaving now. I wished they wouldn't. Not sorry about Droppers though. . . .

"All right," Mulder called out, "we can't be held up by Geerdes' arm any more. We've overwaited as it is. Flashlights straight, toward the ditch. Let me get up front. Let's go. Back to the wives and mothers. Tell 'em what a good time they missed!" And his voice rang out, carrying everywhere, "Hand in hand we go, friends. . . ."

Farther away now, all the voices. Gone, the clump-clumping. Stillness again, just as before. Nothing left to see outside. No moon, not tonight; no stars.

The first free New Year. . . . Last year, what had I done then? Sat upstairs, but with Johan, Dientje, Opoe, Sini. We told each other stories, laughed. Rachel? I hadn't known about her. In her room probably, too, with *her* 'family.' And now? Maybe she was in church. She went all the time now, not just once a year, to a special room, in a wheelchair, women up front—not allowed to look behind at the men in wheelchairs, as the head nurse kept reminding them.

And Sini, where would she be now? Don't know. Opoe, Dientje? Must be home. Johan? On the road with his friends, definitely. Walking into his house, too, now. "Fui-fui, Johan," Opoe would say, shaking her head, "all the noise you made. And just for New Year's. No, that I can't see."

Opoe, Dientje, Sini, Rachel, Johan. "What's Annie doing now?" Were they wondering?

"I'm here," I whispered. I hadn't really thought about them for so long. Hadn't written either. I would, now. Yes, yes. I closed the window, turned on the light, got out pencil, paper. Wrote.

· 8 ·

"You pay in life for everything," people grumbled. "Who needed such a mild summer if it gets followed by this kind of winter?" Their faces were worried as they checked the sky. "More snow coming, I don't care what the paper says. That'll be the fifth storm this winter." And they hurried on, newspapers in their shoes. The soles they had been able to get were thin, and standing in line took a long time.

When they came home, there were other things to worry about. Their roofs, doors, window frames, were repaired, but look at the way it was done, with parts from destroyed houses. Could fall apart any day. . . . Already they could feel a draft. And the coalman came rarely, never brought enough.

"Don't worry," the government comforted everyone. "There will be enough to last all winter. In the meantime here is some advice. Ration your coal at home. It's better to be a little chilly all winter than to freeze before the end of it."

Obediently people put on all the sweaters they could find and huddled closer to their stoves at night, plopping in only a few coals at a time, just enough to keep the fire going.

"Winters don't last forever," they comforted each other—and themselves.

We sat by our stove, too. Father so close that his feet rested against it. Mother's, in slippers, were resting on the footstool. Her elbows were buried in cushions. I smiled. I had put a scarf next to her, neatly folded, for a little later, when the fire went out and it really got cold. She had not seen it yet. She was too busy with the magazine on her lap, turning one page after another, looking at the pictures.

"Annie . . ."

From the other end of the sofa I looked up, hopefully. Had she noticed it? "Yes, Mother?"

"I'm so glad I sent Nel all those warm things, before I even knew it would get this cold. She must be nice and snug."

I nodded. Yes.

"The fun she must be having. Leave it to her. She knows what she wants, and what really counts." The hand stopped. "She's getting it, Annie. That's wonderful. How many people can say that?"

Only one pale yellow flame was left in the stove, slowly licking at a single coal.

"Annie . . ."

"What?"

"At least life is turning out to be exciting for one of us. It's lucky she's the one." A little edgy now. "And it doesn't matter to me that she has no time for other things or even other people. That's all right, I guess. That's the way it should be." Noisily Mother exchanged the magazine for her nail file. "This wind, it has not stopped howling for weeks. In Amsterdam you don't have to just sit and listen to it. You don't notice those things when you have somewhere to go."

Gray and dusty, the coals; powdery, the ashes. The room was getting chilly. She could use the scarf now. I pushed it closer to her. "Here, put it on." Anxiously I watched her. She didn't want to? No. She was giving it back.

"Don't you know wool scarves never go on sofas? I didn't teach you that. You only wear them when you're outside."

I blushed, quickly got up, put it back in the hall. So hard to know what to do these days, or to say. Like the other evening, when I'd mentioned that Sini hardly ever wrote, either, or telephoned, just like Nel. It wasn't the same, Mother said. She'd been angry.

I sighed, checked the clock. Five more minutes. . . . Should I go to the kitchen now? Maybe she'd like that. Then Father would stop reading sooner. No, I'd better go at exactly the right time.

Perhaps now it was time. Quietly I went to the kitchen, turned on the faucet, held the kettle underneath it.

No more walks at night, after the book. Too cold. Tea instead, all three of us. With talk about cows, money, what we'd do with it.

"I'll buy a car, Magda, so I can do more business."

"Visit Nel, Ies."

"And see Rachel," Father added quickly. "Annie could come with us."

With Rachel we'd wait, Mother thought. "She's not going to leave the sanatorium in such a hurry anyway."

But we could not get a car, Father had said later, not for a long time. He had sounded a little relieved. There still weren't enough for all the doctors, who really needed them.

It would have been nice to visit Rachel, to sit with her. . . . I suppose Mother was right though. I checked the water. Not boiling yet. I could do something else while I waited. I got out the pail, small shovel, screen, so Father could sift the ashes later and pick out the pieces of coal that were large enough to save, to add to tomorrow night's fire.

It was colder, even more bitter than before. Icy winds blew, coming in through cracks in doors, window frames, roofs, penetrating through layers of clothing. "What have we done to deserve this," people agonized. "No matter what we do, we freeze."

The coalman hardly came at all. There was no wood either. When it was dark, many doors opened up all over Holland, just a little, and out sneaked people, saws in hand, to cut down trees, the way they had during the war. "What else can we do?" they whispered to each other, arms already moving. "We have to fend for ourselves. The government gives us nothing."

Not only in Holland was the winter bitterly cold. Over much of Europe, it was the same. In Germany, in Nuremberg.

When the papers arrived with the latest reports of the twenty-one men, the people of Holland were furious. "Look at them," they yelled, pointing stiff fingers at the pictures. "You don't see them sitting with blankets wrapped around them. In shirtsleeves yet. Justice," they sneered. "A waste of food and good coal—that's what it is"

Many people were sick, and doctors had trouble making house calls. It was too cold and slippery for their bicycles, and there was not enough gas for

those who had cars. The roads v   y. Only a
few buses ran, to important c   they did
not stop in Usselo. The gas. . . .

Shivering, the people, sta   feet.
"Warm boots we need." "T   us
with socks." "Coats we want." "Abundance, abundance. Whoever said that was lying. The only
thing we've got plenty of is bad weather."
"Haven't had a decent thing to eat since Christmas." "Now's when we could use it." "A bowl of
pea soup. . . ."

Then, one evening, the queen spoke. We should
be brave, she said. "This winter will pass too, just as
all the other unpleasant things have passed."

"Well," people said sheepishly, "if the queen
says so. . . ." They looked ashamed, almost.

With us, nothing had changed. Johan wrote. So
did Rachel, and Sini, occasionally. There was
school; going to the masseur. I was putting on
too much weight, he said. But Mother still didn't
think I ate enough. I ran home, though, every
afternoon.

"Did you see the mailman, Annie?" Mother
would greet me from the sofa. "I might have missed
him."

She hadn't. A new magazine was on the table.

"I'm happy, Annie," she said. "I'm not worried, or I'd call. Nel can take care of herself. I taught her well."

"Yes, Mother." Carefully, I sat down, trying not to wrinkle the cushions. Mother was silent. She didn't look as happy as she said she was. Maybe I could cheer her up. How? Put on the potatoes? A little early still. I could suggest it though. "Mother?"

No, not yet. Just as I had thought. But she smiled, a little. Nice.

And on the winter went, on, in the same way. Until. . . .

"Annie, come here fast. The wonderful places she's gone to, the things she's done. I told you. . . ."

Look how happy she is, just holding Nel's letter. Slowly I followed Mother into the house.

· 9 ·

Already the air smelled different, lighter, and the wind had lost its bite. Each day more snow was melting. Grass . . . could see it again. Crocuses began to push up, green tips that grew, opened up, became purple and yellow. Birds returned, dots in the sky that grew bigger and bigger. They landed and began to sing the minute it became light in the morning.

In a small hollow outside a town somewhere in Holland, a fisherman saw the first plover's eggs, four of them, spotted, green and black. And in age-old tradition they were given to the queen to show her that spring had come. "It took long enough," people said, but they were laughing and spending as much time outside as possible again.

That's where I would go—out—as soon as this class was over. Wednesday . . . only half a day of school. I took another look out the window. So blue, the sky, only a few feathery patches of clouds, puffy ones, that moved, moved.

Finally, the bell rang. I ran as the others were doing, not caring whether Mr. Klaver yelled, "Whoever is in a hurry comes back." Outside the door I sighed with relief. He hadn't.

Was someone calling?

"Annie, wait for me. No one else is going my way."

Selma? Going home alone? Must be. She was saying good-bye to her friends. "See you later, everybody," turning to this one and that. I'd stand right here, where she could see me. "Selma?" She hadn't heard, but it didn't matter. I wouldn't let her go without me.

Where was she? Still at it, I saw. "Bye, Kees . . . see you . . . see you . . . see you." Waving, walking backward. Well, she couldn't go on forever. First time I'd be alone with her. Maybe it would be nice. She might be different by herself. Now I could get to know her better. Not just anybody either, Selma . . . popular. She was coming. I picked up my schoolbag, held it tightly. Now then.

Timidly I walked next to her. I should say something, shouldn't I? She was used to that. About school, that would be easy. Did she think Mr. Klaver was mean?

"Uh-huh."

"When he handed out those papers. . . ."

"Uh-huh, same with me."

Peculiar answer. I glanced at her. She was smiling to herself almost as if she were miles away. "Selma, I thought we wouldn't get that test till . . ."

"You won't believe what's happened to me. I'm going steady." She paused.

"Going steady?" My goodness!

"It happened yesterday, at the post office, as I was about to go in for stamps. I said to him, 'I can't decide here on the steps. This is too big a decision; give me at least till tomorrow.' He wouldn't. 'Two minutes,' he said, 'that's all.'

"He kept looking at his watch; he really meant it. I almost fainted. So what could I do? I said yes. It's a great responsibility though. I don't know whether I'm ready for it. See you tomorrow, Annie."

Baffled, I stared after her. She hadn't even told me whom she was going steady with. Kees? Who knew? Could be anybody. I crossed the railroad tracks. They were no longer rusty. Too many trains going over, polishing them. It had been kind of interesting, what she said, I had to admit. She wasn't any different though from when I had heard her with the others. Same Selma—boys, boys, boys. I couldn't listen to that dumb stuff all the time. I had more important things to do. Home, quickly, into the garden; see whether the pink hyacinth had opened.

Mother was in the garden. She looked very serious. I'd better not disturb her. She must be thinking of what else to plant when the gardener came. I'd go right in, bring the potatoes out, and watch. They were waiting for me on the sink, with the knife I needed.

I settled down on the grass, chose a potato from the pile, and began. Longer and longer the peel grew, curly, thin. We had gone shopping yesterday, Mother and I—for a skirt. We went as soon as we heard about them, before they were all gone.

"How are you, Magda?" Mr. de Wind had said,

coming over to us immediately. And then he asked which one of the ladies he could help. Me! I almost rushed ahead of him to the rack. Skirts, a whole row of them. Beautiful . . . blue. I couldn't wait to try one on.

Mr. de Wind measured me, handed me one. I stepped into it. So nice and soft. It wouldn't button though, no matter what I did: hold in my stomach, stop breathing.

"I don't understand," Mother said to Mr. de Wind. "I never had that problem with Nel. You remember? It was as if the designer had her figure in mind. Hold your stomach in, Annie, and let me see."

I tried on several more.

"Don't worry," Mother told Mr. de Wind. "It's not your fault. We can't expect them to make skirts to fit every size."

We left. There was no point in looking anywhere else either, Mother said. We had gone to another store anyway, where they had material. Gray, but almost a little blue—if you looked at it a certain way. And we got other things—thread, buttons, everything. The skirt would be beautiful. Mother sewed well. She had already let out my clothes, couldn't even tell where. She used to sew for Nel when they had nothing in the stores they liked. Mother had not wanted to make clothes again, didn't enjoy it any more. But she was going to do it, though it would be a lot of work. She didn't even complain about it, just said I didn't have an easy figure. Kept changing.

Slowly I picked up another potato. So big. I glared at it. Thicker the peels. Shorter the curls. She'd never notice. Father took them to the cows anyway.

Footsteps on the road. "Broekman, here" came Mother's voice. "By the hedge."

It was the gardener, his arms full of plants. "We can get started right away, Mrs. de Leeuw, and I'll try not to take any longer than I have to," he promised. But after every plant he put in, he slowly straightened his back. "A little bit of rest does a lot of good, Mrs. de Leeuw," he explained, "especially in the spring when the ground doesn't give."

"If it helps the garden." Mother laughed.

"It does," he assured her, still stretching.

"Good afternoon, Mrs. de Leeuw. Hi, Annie. What pretty things are going on here," Maria called. "Come, Sweetie, let's take a look." Nudging her goat on with her knee, she came over. "Oh, oh, oh, I was right," she marveled, leaning across the hedge. "When they've got those contests again, Mrs. de Leeuw, I bet your garden will get all the ribbons."

Mother liked that. "Thank you," she said. "And it will be all right if you want to come by every day and watch the progress."

"We will, we will." Maria beamed, lovingly looking down at her goat. "Watch where you eat," she scolded it. "That hedge has thorns. You know you can't take those. What am I going to do with you? Come."

"How can anyone love an animal that much?" Mother said wonderingly, looking after them. "All they do is make a mess. Broekman," she hinted, "I don't like paying for leaning on shovels either."

Instantly the soil began to fly again. A few more plants went in, same way, with rests on the shovel in between. Mother was joking now. Nice. Didn't do that too often.

Maybe she didn't want him to quit. There weren't that many gardeners, and he was a good one. Worked at the best places in town, Mother said. "As soon as you can, Broekman, I'd like azaleas, anemones, chrysanthemums."

"I will, Mrs. de Leeuw. Get you some fine ones, too, and I'll see you next week."

I smiled. Mother certainly knew how to handle him.

She was walking around again, I saw, touching the evergreen that had been there for years, a shrub with leaves just unfolding. She stopped in

front of the forsythia bush. Carefully she pulled a
branch closer, inspected it, then eased it back, not
disturbing the flowers at all. She stepped back,
admired it again.

They were beautiful, even yellower than when I
had gone to school this morning. "It's such a nice
bush, Mother."

She turned around. "That shows good taste,
Annie."

Confused I nodded. A compliment? Yes, definitely. I got to my feet, picked up the pail, the basket
with peels—thick ones and thin.

"If you had any talent," Mother continued, "you
could make a picture of it and keep it forever."
Briskly she went in.

"Good taste," she had said. After all these
months . . . Father had been right. "Patience,
Annie, and it'll all come." I looked at the forsythia
bush once more, fondly. Then, lightly, I went in.
You have good taste, she said. Good taste, good
taste. . . .

Part Four

SPRING

The weather held. One sunny day ran into another, as if trying to make up for lost time. The roads were crowded again with cars and hitchhikers. "How far can you take us? How far?" There were buses again, going in all directions this time, and stopping in many towns, no matter how small.

"Good-bye, Mother." I stood in the doorway. I had already said good-bye to Father a while ago, before he left for work. "Have a nice time," he had wished me. "And give my love to the Oostervelds."

I would. In less than two hours. Would Mother say it, too?

I looked at her. She was still getting dressed. She was wearing jewelry today, and a silk scarf. Pretty.

"Annie, . . ."

Instantly I let go of the doorknob.

"That pleat in the front doesn't please me," she said, frowning, pulling at it a little, "but it's definitely not my sewing. They'll like it. They'll know I take good care of you."

"Yes, Mother."

"Annie, . . ."

"Yes, Mother?" Now she'd say it.

"Be sure to change into your old skirt when you get there."

Of course. Nothing to worry about.

Intently Mother was combing her hair, trying to swirl the waves this way, that way; different today.

I waited another second. She was still combing. . . .

Slowly I reached the road. I turned around to look at the house, the garden. In less than an hour Nel would come. Easter vacation for her, too.

In town the day had also begun. Bedding was hanging across windowsills, to air. In the Misterstraat the first of the new windows in the stores were being washed. With long, careful strokes, Mr. de Wind moved a sponge across his window. "Doesn't it look wonderful," he called over to his neighbor. "I have only three more boards to get rid of. By Christmas I'll be all set. The government promised."

Near them a woman was sweeping the sidewalk. Her broom was stiff and scratchy—also new. Other sounds in the street; the milkman's bell as he made his rounds. Customers rushed over to his cart

with a pot, a coupon. In the marketplace the farmers had already set up their stands and were calling
attention to their wares. "Look 'ere, look 'ere." I
stopped. So many flowers—purples, yellows, reds,
all of those in one; pansies, spilling over the side of
the pails.

Bong, bong. I'd better hurry, run. At the bus
stop I joined the end of the line. I was just in time.
The sound of the horn, loud and hoarse, came from
around the corner. The line began to move.

· 2 ·

The bus was full of people going on vacation, or
visiting just for the day. Someone across from me
was talking about that.

"After supper tonight we can come home, wife.
Not like the other time, remember? We stood on
the road waiting for a car so long that we had to
turn around and sleep at the kids' house after all?
And the dog kept us up all night?"

"I'm glad we didn't try that again," his wife
grumbled. "Driver, you're sure now about the
return schedule?" Relaxed, she leaned back.

We were no longer in Winterswijk. We had
reached the main road. I looked at my suitcase.

Mother's. It was an old one, a little scratched. Carefully I moved it out from under my neighbor's feet.

We were already in Groenlo, I saw, and nearly through it. Only a few houses now along a narrow street. Then nothing but the road again.

Nel—closer and closer. . . . I even knew what stop her train was at now—Zutphen. "And once she's there, Annie, it's almost as if she's home already." I sighed. I didn't want to think about that. Johan and Dientje—I hadn't seen them in so long, not since the wedding. And Opoe—even longer than that. It would be nice. I wouldn't have to walk just so, eat just so, sit . . . not always have to think of what to do next.

Just be with them . . . be me. They might have left their house already, could even be at the bus stop now, waiting for me. I'd make sure I'd be the first one off. I glanced out the window. Not there yet. Another village to go. Now almost. Quickly I walked to the front of the bus to remind the driver. "Usselo?" he repeated. "Not too many calls for that place." I got off. I was the only one.

· 3 ·

Where were Johan and Dientje? For a second I stood still, thinking. Maybe they had not been able to figure out the time. Sure, with my handwriting? Well, I'd get there myself. I began to walk down the road.

"Hi." I waved back at a man on a cart. People were friendly here, and it was so quiet, none of the big town noises Winterswijk had.

There was something new. Where the rubble from the old bakery had been was a shed with a sign, "Good bread and rolls here." And look, in Spieker Diena's store, four different-colored socks were on display, temptingly dangling from a clothesline that was stretched all the way across the window. Faster now. Almost, almost. Right there, the farm, the geranium beds in front of the house. Two people running toward me.

"I told you, Dientje, we can't tell with that clock. She's here already."

"Be careful with her, Johan," Dientje warned. "You just came from the stable."

"Ah, woman," he yelled jubilantly, "she doesn't care. See? She hasn't changed a bit. She's still our little Annie."

Opoe was rushing over, too, laughing and wiping her face on her apron before she offered me her cheek. So wonderful to be back. Now I realized how much I had missed them. Holding their hands, I went in the house.

"She looks tired, Johan." "Not like she used to." "Sit in Ma's chair." "No, not you, Vlekje." "Nice and plump though"—interrupting each other, tripping over their words.

"I see a real figure on'r." Opoe came closer to get a better look.

"And the skirt—beautiful."

"I got something new, too, Annie." Dientje beamed. "I'll show you later, after we eat." "How are your father, and, and your"—rapidly she hurried on—"mother? That's good, that's good." On, right away. "D'you have friends?"

"Sort of," I said hesitantly. The walk home with Selma. . . .

"Ah, friends, I want to hear about learning. How are you doing with those formulas we talked about?"

"Physics?" I laughed. "Horrible, Johan."

"The calf Annie—Annie, now that you're here it sounds so funny calling her that—she's something. Frisky." Johan made his hands leap in the air. "I'll show you later."

I nodded vigorously.

"I've got so much to tell you, Annie. Can't put it all in a letter."

"I know, Johan. But they were fine letters." Not like this though—one piece of news after another, with Opoe and Dientje making sure he didn't forget anything.

"Johan, tell her about the minister," Dientje urged.

"Goddammit, Annie. Yes. Remember, since the parsonage got bombed he's been living with people down the road? And he couldn't stand their cooking? Ja, that I wrote. Well—" He paused, rubbed his nose, and settled his feet more comfortably on another chair. "One day Mr. Hannink came here and said, 'You take him. It's only for a couple of days. Then he'll go to someone else's house.'

"I said to him, 'That's the same thing you told us when you brought Annie and Sini, and look how long that lasted. That was wonderful, but I'm not sure I can stand having a minister underfoot.'"

"With the way Johan talks sometimes, Annie, we weren't sure the minister would put up with us."

I giggled.

"Ja, she knows, woman, I don't hide anything. But I said, 'Let'm come for an evening. I'll try him out.' I did, Annie. Nothing bothered him, nothing.

Couldn't tell he was a minister except for looking at him. Ha, ha, three weeks he stayed. That Mr. Hannink always fools us."

"And he ate"—Opoe shook her head—"as if he did real work."

"He liked what I cooked, Annie. And we don't eat out of the pan any more. Regular plates we're using, and all the time the way you do in Winterswijk, not just for birthdays." Dientje's face looked flushed.

"That couldn't be helped," Opoe said gravely, "with a minister in the house."

"Ja, ja." Johan laughed. "Many fellow—er, er, mankind have passed through my house. Jews, Germans, Canadians, and now the minister. I said that nicely, Annie, didn't I?" Johan said triumphantly. "Fellow mankind? Ja, ja, I learn easy enough, even though I never did go to school much —English, church talk, everything."

"Johan, that Willem—"

"Ja, Ma, I'm getting there. Remember him, Annie? He was picked up on Liberation Day? He's out of jail again and back on his farm. That's how it goes. Came home looking good, too. Had a nice rest, I guess. And everyone in Usselo talks to him again. 'Life goes on,' they say. 'We've got to forget.' But me"—Johan raised his voice—"I still hate him, that traitor. I wouldn't say good morning to'm even if he said it to me."

"And Johan, tell'r about the crime Usselo had."

"Can you believe, a bag of nails disappeared from Berend's shed. And who did it still isn't saying."

"Annie looks exhausted from all the news." They laughed. "That tiny Usselo, eh? Ja, ja, not everything happens just in big towns."

The door opened. A woman came in, tittering. Leida, who else?

"Hiya, everyone. I bet Annie doesn't recognize me now that I've got teeth."

"I do." I laughed.

"They don't work, Annie; they only look good. I can't wear them when I eat. They hurt so. I should take'm back to that dentist to complain, but every time I sit down in his chair he wants something else from me before he begins. Last time it was a ham. They say I should go to the police, but I hate to do that."

"Yes, yes." Understandingly everyone nodded.

"Well"—Leida was smiling again—"if you're finished with the paper, I'll take it, Johan. Ever since the war, we all read the news in Usselo." She giggled. "We don't want to be surprised again. I've got a radio, but who's in the house long enough to sit and listen to it? Annie's looking at the date of the paper." She roared. "Three days old, she thinks, and Leida here calls it news. Johan, I've got to run. You tell'r we want to know what's going on, but we don't want to spend the money on it, so we all share."

Sheepishly Johan looked at me. Leida stuck her head back in. "Annie, I'll see you. I suppose you're staying for a while."

"She sure is," Johan answered, "through Easter at least. She's got to help us eat the eggs, Leida."

I'd like to. . . . The door closed again. Leida's laughter faded and was gone. There was something I had to say. "Johan," I began.

"How many eggs can you eat this year, Annie? Six, eh? Ha, more I bet. Eight? Dientje, maybe a couple of dozen like me."

I had to tell them. Couldn't wait any longer. I blurted it out. "I won't be here on Sunday." They stared, all three of them; didn't believe me. I said it again, "I won't be here—" I swallowed, waited.

"When?" Johan demanded.

His face. . . . Couldn't look at him. "Thursday," I whispered.

Now he knew. His voice. "Did you hear that, Ma, Dientje? Goddammit, Annie, you can't do that. You've got to stay longer."

I shook my head. I couldn't.

"Why not."

I closed my eyes—Mother. "What d'you want to go to Usselo for? You just saw them in October. That should be enough for anyone. Well, if you want to, go ahead, for four days.

Johan's voice again. "Tell me."

"So much work to do for school," I whispered.

"And maybe her mother will miss'r if she stays longer. Right, Annie?" Anxiously Dientje looked at me.

Grateful, I nodded. Yes, that was it.

But Johan was still upset. "She has her all the time. We've talked about you all winter, Annie. You don't know. Wait till she comes, we kept saying. Can't be later than Eastertime. And we'll sit around the table and eat eggs like we did a couple of years in a row. Sini can't be here. That we understand. But you. . . ."

Please, Johan, no more. I can't stand it.

"Nothing ever goes the way it should. Never has, either. Before the war, I didn't notice. Now I see it."

"God-o-god-o-god, Johan, enough." Heavily Opoe got up, looked for something in the cabinet, found it. Cups. "Fui-fui, that Annie must think we've got nothing to drink here."

Silence. Only Dientje's fingers rubbing the table back and forth. Even that sound stopped. She got up, went to the stove, reached for the coffeepot.

"I hope you made it right this time," Opoe said, "not watery as you usually do." Dientje winked and poured me a cup anyway. Timidly I looked at Johan. He put his hand on mine, squeezed it.

"I know it's not your fault. I just got carried away." He picked up his cup, drank. I did, too. Relaxing, all of us again, and talking; but nice talk now, not like the other. I snuggled deeper into Opoe's easy chair and swung my legs across the arm.

"Happy you're here?" Dientje asked.

Yes. The begonias on the windowsill, the kettle on the stove, hissing a little just as it always did. Yes.

Noon dinner was over. The plates were waiting by the pump to be washed. "Annie, want me to show you now?" With a red face Dientje hurried ahead of me up the stairs. "I have it in the closet" —she stopped and looked proudly at me over her shoulder—"on a hanger." She rushed into her bedroom, opened the closet door, and gingerly lifted something out. "It's a dress. What d'you think of it, Annie? Tell me honestly."

"I like it, Dientje. It has such a nice pocket."

"Yes, doesn't it?" She wriggled her hand into it. "You can tell it's lace, can't you?"

"Yes, and those buttons."

"Aren't they pretty?" Dientje agreed. "They're different, you see that? They're not round, and they're shiny? Spieker's Diena has beautiful things, Annie." Lovingly Dientje's hands slid down the skirt. "It took an awful lot of coupons, mine and most of Opoe's," she whispered, listening for footsteps on the stairs. "Don't tell 'em. I know it isn't exactly what your mother had on at the wedding, Annie, but it's a little like it, you think?"

"It matches your eyes, Dientje."

Shyly she looked at me. "Ja, kind of blue, right? I can't wait till I have some place to go, so I can wear it. And I can say to people, it's almost like Mrs. de Leeuw's dress." Carefully she hung it back in the closet. "I'm learning things, too, Annie. Just like Johan."

I closed the stable door behind me. "See you later, Johan." Maybe I'd take a tiny rest, for a few minutes, no more. I knew exactly where, a wonderful place—in the apple tree along the side of the house, the one with the low branch that looked like a bench. One more peek in the chicken coop . . . in the kitchen . . . still doing the laundry.

I sat down. Comfortable; pretty, too. Blossoms

everywhere, above my head, around, almost on my head . . . closed most of them . . . red . . . I leaned back, carefully stretched out my legs. Almost straight again. Soon no one would ever be able to tell they had been crooked. I began to whistle, a French tune about a garden, like this one . . . trees.

There were so many things to look at. The whole side of the house, the shed, the stable, the chicken coop, the gate to my right, even a little bit of the road beyond. And the meadow—I just had to turn my head a little, and there was the calf tied to a post. That frisky.

"The cows were glad to get out, too, Annie. Don't kid yourself, they get tired of standing in the same spot all winter." There, the special cow with the one black ear, had crossed the meadow again, udder swaying.

We had a talk about the cow, Johan and I, in the stable. "She's been giving so much milk," he said, excited. "Five extra guilders worth last week, and I'm putting it all away. Guess for what? A tractor. You know what I'm going to do with it? Every-one's work. Piet's, Koos's, and all the others' who don't want to do it themselves. Yep. They'll ask me, you'll see. Ahh, before you know it I'll be driving around all the fields, sitting down, getting paid for it, too. I'll be an important man." He grinned. "I bet they'll say, 'That Johan, what he can't do!'" He picked up the pitchfork, pushed it back into the dirty straw, looked at me. "Don't say anything about it to Dientje though. She'll think I'm crazy. I'll get to it when I'm ready."

The door of the chicken coop opened. Opoe came out, holding the basket of eggs in one hand, cleaning rag in the other. She must have had a good day; her face was all crinkly with laughter. "Fifteen of 'em, Annie."

Dientje had also finished her work. She was standing in the kitchen doorway, smiling. Wisps of wet hair stuck out from under her kerchief. She picked up the milking jugs.

Time now for Johan to bring the cows in for the night. Yes, there he was already, walking straight through the grass to the special one. He must be anxious to start milking that one first, see how much. . . . "Coming, Johan." Eagerly I jumped down. Me, too.

What about today though? Watch them again? I already had yesterday, all day, almost from the minute I got up. "C'mon, Annie, over here. I'm going to wash the cows' tails." Five of them. And in the shed, cutting up potatoes for planting, a bushel at least. I had helped. Dientje had not even wanted me to. "You should enjoy yourself while you're here, Annie."

I looked out the kitchen window. Maybe I'd go outside? Sit? Maybe so. It was early still. The tree was a little damp. With a corner of my skirt I dabbed the branch. A few blossoms had opened, all white now. And some, almost open, that one by my knee, maybe even by tonight in this weather. Wherever I looked, the sky was blue. I sighed, settled myself a little better. The green of the kitchen door looked different today, darker; so did the stable and the strips of the chicken coop. I strained my eyes. Yes, the paint on the shed too, same thing, pretty. The branches and twigs were moving, making tiny sounds. Hardly any from the road. A horse sometimes, a cart going up the road, to Piet's farm, or down the road, past Koos's. A cow being taken to a meadow. Shovel sounds from the stable. Sweeping ones from the coop. I shut my eyes, opened them again. Something had changed. The sun was beginning to stick up above the shed, and there, near me, a tiny bug was climbing up a blade of grass. Long this morning, actually, very long. Maybe I should go for the walk again, stop at Spieker's Diena for a while, see whether she had something new in the window, go as far as the baker. Walk slowly. I brushed my shoes across a cluster of tall weeds. Later.

"Having a good time, Annie?" Dientje was on her way to the stable.

"Yes." I smiled. She did not have to worry.

Cheerfully she walked on. I would have liked to ask her whether or not she still thought Mother missed me. I had been gone for days now. Was she outside, too, in the garden with Nel? Maybe they were talking about me at this very moment. "I couldn't have gotten a better daughter, Nel. She's wonderful. Learned so quickly. Never gives me any trouble. I don't even understand it myself, because there was a lot she didn't know. I wish it was Thursday already, so she'd be home. You should see her now."

I slid down from the tree and went into the kitchen. I picked up the paper, put it down again. I glanced at Opoe's chair, the one they called easy. Hesitantly I walked into the good room. Everything did look good in here. Only if ever they had more than twenty people visiting, they wouldn't know where to put them. Restlessly I wandered on, up the stairs. The doors to the bedrooms were open. I walked into Johan and Dientje's. The furniture . . . no carvings on anything, just wood and who knew from where? From trees in Usselo probably.

Look how their bed was made. Covers all wrong.
Their feet would stick out in no time, touch the
footboard, could make smudges. And the curtain
—it had been opened just like that. Uneven, puckered. No thought to it. Had it always been like
that?

Slowly I walked into the back room, where Sini
and I had spent so much time. What was the matter
with me today, walking around, inspecting? If it
hadn't been for Johan and Dientje, I might not
even be here. They'd taken us in just like that, had
never even seen us. "We've got the space, Dientje.
We can't let them get killed. They're just kids."
That bed—I had slept in it with them, all those
years. And Sini, on the floor, close, too. So we'd be
safe. Live.

I stared out the window. Coop, shed, stable. The
wheelbarrow standing next to it—rusty. I stopped,
bent my head, ashamed. It was the same wheelbarrow Johan had taken us out in that day, after we'd
been in hiding for two years. We'd gone to the
field all the way in the back so we'd get some sun,
see the sky, be like other people, a little. Nice. That
had been then though—a long time ago. What
about now? Special place, this. And the people in it
. . . special too. Would stay that way. Always.
Only . . . hard to be here now. So many voices in
my head. Johan and Dientje's, Mother's. Didn't

know which one to listen to. Home, tomorrow.
Can't wait. Nicer there. No smell of cows. . . .
Things for me to do. I got up, walked to the door.
Maybe I would watch Johan and Dientje again.
They'd like that.

"Let's sit in the good room tonight," Dientje
said.

"She's showing off, Annie." Johan laughed.

We went in, the four of us. We were not laughing any more; not talking either. Dientje's hands
were folded in her lap. Johan sat quietly, smoking.
There, Opoe was going to say something.

"We've got to try a different spot for the cabbage, Johan. They grew scrawny, like sprouts,
where we had 'em."

Somberly he crushed out his cigarette. "I know,
Ma."

Opoe was studying the edge of her apron. "Let's
have something to eat," she finally suggested.
Quickly Dientje got up and went to the kitchen.

"Cut four nice pieces," Opoe called out. Then to
me, "We've saved part of a cake. Dientje didn't
make it. The baker did." Instantly Vlekje came out
from under Opoe's chair, stood up against it, pawed
her. "You can't have any," she said regretfully.
"It's too good. Don't forget you're a dog.

"Dientje," she called in to the kitchen again,

"where are the cookies you baked?" Opoe's hand patted Vlekje's head. "They were too hard for me, but maybe she'll let you eat one."

Silence again. Slowly I began on my cake. Opoe was softening hers under her tongue.

"You like it, right?" Dientje nodded to me.

"Yes." I took another bite, a bigger one. Johan had not touched his. My eyes wandered to what was in the middle of the table, a basket holding a bundle of letters tied together with string.

Dientje noticed. "You know which one's in there, Annie? The first one you wrote to us, telling us how well things worked out between you and your mother. Johan and I were so worried about you. I cried, Annie, on the way home from the wedding. I said to Johan, 'What's going to happen to her?' She made you do all the work." Dientje fingered the package. "A lot of these letters are yours, Annie."

"Ja, ja, the mailman's here all the time these days." Johan was cheering up. "As if I've got an office. One day, during New Year's, we had two letters at once. I'm not kidding. I had to bring the fellow in here. Show him the photographs again, prove it." He pointed to the chest along the wall. "Ha, ha, he never came before the war. Remember, Ma? Except to bring the tax bill."

"Every winter, Johan. And he'd say, 'Coffee ready?' and sit for a while. Two cups, I remember."

But not like now, Mother." Dientje laughed.

"No," Opoe conceded, "now he has business here all the time." Solemnly she stared at what was left of her cake.

Again no one said anything. The only sounds came from Vlekje. He was chewing the cookies. Then he went back under the chair, became still, too.

"We haven't heard from Sini for a long time," Dientje said, breaking the silence. "She must be forgetting us." She laughed nervously.

"Of course not, Dientje," Johan flared up. "What a thing to say. When she was a nurse in Enschede, she came to visit all the time. She's very, very busy."

"Running around, if you ask me." Opoe pursed her lips.

"Goddammit, Ma, that's not true," Johan said in an angry voice. "Those kids she's taking care of keep her going day and night. That's why we haven't heard from her. One of them is under a year, can't even stand yet. We've got it in a letter." He jumped up, took the string off the bundle, and looked through the letters. "Here it is." In a loud voice he began to read: "I may not even stay that much longer. I have to work so hard that I have no time for anything else." Triumphantly he looked at Opoe.

"Besides"—here his voice became a little hesitant—"I haven't been able to find one Jewish boy I like." Abruptly he stopped. "I guess that's it." He tied the string around the bundle again. "Forgetting us," he muttered. "Dumb talk. After what we went through together?"

Uneasily I fidgeted on my chair. Too early to go to bed yet.

"They could become strangers, Johan, with Sini off in a big city and Annie in that fancy house."

"So what, woman? Won't make any difference, not between us and the girls."

"You're awfully quiet, Annie." Worriedly Dientje looked at Johan. "She used to talk much more during the war, remember?"

"And giggle," Opoe added. "Fui-fui, all the time."

"Sit on my lap." Johan laughed. "I couldn't keep'r off. Like the devil, the minute I came upstairs, she'd climb on."

"On mine, too, Johan," Dientje reminded him.

"Tell about the first time the girls came here during the war, Johan," Opoe said eagerly.

He jumped up and pretended he was me. He stuck out a hand and said in an elegant voice, "How do you do, Mrs. Oosterveld.' The look on your face, Ma. None of us knew what she wanted with that hand. She didn't know what a bunch of dumb peasants she had come to that only shake hands at weddings and funerals." Johan laughed so hard he had to wipe the tears from his eyes. "We had a nice war, Annie. That, I must say." Roughly he shoved his handkerchief back in his pocket. When he spoke again, it was hard to understand him. "We were a real family, then. We had kids."

On the other side of the room, next to their wedding picture, hung the photographs of Sini and me, smiling.

"I think we'd better leave now, Annie."

"Not yet, Johan," Dientje protested. "It only takes you two minutes to get there. She doesn't want to hang around that bus stop for an hour."

Johan checked the clock again, frowned. "There's no saying what time it really is. You can't trust an antique. Besides, I'm not going to leave her there alone."

"I want to come, Johan," Dientje said.

Firmly he shook his head. "That wouldn't be right, not the way people in Usselo talk. 'Look at 'em,' they'd say, 'they're both going off as if they've got nothing better to do, and it's a work-day.' Now, that, we can't do."

Wistfully Dientje looked at him. "You think so?"

"For sure." He gulped the rest of his coffee down.

"Here, Annie." Opoe came into the kitchen. "For your Easter Sunday." Looking mysterious, she gave me a bag. "Don't open it till you get home. But they're nice and fresh, cleaned off and every-thing."

"I'll be careful not to break them, Opoe." Awk-wardly I stood there, waiting. Shouldn't we go?

But Dientje was talking about the next time. "We'll take'r somewhere, Johan. On a Sunday, and we'll both go, right after milking."

A real conversation, Johan sitting down again. "We could easily enough. I've already thought about it. I've even picked the place."

"The waterwheel on the other side of Usselo, Johan. Right?"

"Sure, Ma." Now Johan was pulling out his tobacco tin and hunting around for his cigarette paper. "It's got big paddles, Annie. You won't believe what you see. People go there these days just to look, they tell me. Stay for hours. Healthy there. Cool, too . . . breezy."

"They sell lemonade, I hear. I'll get her a glass. . . ."

"We could all have some."

"And I'll wear my new dress, the new one," Dientje said.

"If you're going to be that fancy, woman, I'll have to wear the suit." They looked at me, all of them. "You'd better come back soon, Annie. We've got great plans."

I nodded.

Finally Johan picked up my suitcase. "Come."

Dientje took my face between her hands. "You're sorry you have to go home, Annie?" Without waiting for an answer, she went on. "I know, you can't help it. You promised'r. But you weren't bored here?" Her voice trembled.

I shook my head and kissed her. Then I kissed Opoe.

"Make sure you have the bag, Annie."

I held it up for her to see.

"I put something else in it." She chuckled. "For the trip . . . with big pats of butter . . . bread." She came closer. "I can still hug you. I may never be able to again, as old as I am."

Don't say that, Opoe. Please.

At the gate I turned. She was holding Vlekje.

· 4 ·

Arm in arm, Johan and I began to walk, slowly. Wherever I looked, fields. The rye was already up, blades of green as tall as a hand, growing close together, rippling in the wind. There were black stretches, where the soil had just been turned up, and other parts still covered with weeds. A farmer was pushing his plow through those. "C'mon, horse, get a move," he yelled.

"That's Piet, Annie. You talked to him this summer."

I had. I remembered.

"Say hello to'm, Annie."

What if the bus came? "He's busy, Johan." Anxiously I looked down the road.

"Nonsense. He's got all day. Look, he's close to the road now. C'mon, it won't take long." With his elbow he nudged me toward Piet.

Piet put down the handle of the plow and scanned the sky. "Morning," Johan called out. "How goes?"

"Johan, d'you think the good weather will last, or what?"

Johan turned to me. "What do you think, Annie?"

"She came to visit you, I see."

"She sure did." Johan beamed. "For close to a week. It's awfully nice, Piet, to have one of the kids around, let me tell you. I guess she can't forget us. What d'you say?"

"She shouldn't, Johan, not after what you did for her."

"My life, I risked for them. More a person can't do, Piet." He waited.

Piet said no more about it. He'd gone on to something else. "The wife's cousin broke the leg in two places. They had to take'r to the hospital. Not easy to have to go to the city and see'r, with the potatoes coming up."

"No, no, Piet, life isn't easy. Hard work, that's all."

"Well—" Piet spat on his hands, rubbed them together, and picked up the plow again.

"Come, Annie," Johan said quietly.

Was he thinking that Piet used to call him a hero? I put my arm through his.

At the bus stop Johan put my suitcase down. His back was turned to me when he began to speak. "When's the next time, you think?"

I swallowed. "I don't know."

He turned around, took my hand. "You're not mad at me for yelling at you when you first came, are you?"

"No, Johan. Of course not."

"Because I wouldn't want that. I like it, Annie, even when you come for just one day." Hopefully he looked at me. "You think in a few weeks?"

"I'll try." I didn't meet his eyes.

"If you can't, you can't. There's still the whole summer. No school then, eh?" He squeezed my hand. "You're upset, I can see that. Don't think any more about what Dientje said last night. Makes no difference that you go back to Father and Mother or what—fancy house or what—where you are. We'll always love each other. We've gone through too much together, Annie." He stopped, then said carefully, "Don't worry about friends, either. You'll get them, a nice girl like you."

From the left, far away still, the bus. We stood, Johan and I, close. Bigger, the bus. Here it was. My free hand shot up.

Johan's voice was toneless. "You get on now." But he was still holding my hand.

The door opened.

"Go, go."

My hand . . . I put one foot on the step.

"See you soon, Annie. Tell your father and mother to bring you next time and stay for the day. Maybe they'd like that."

The door closed.

"Remember me to them. Bye, Annie, bye. Take care of yourself."

I looked out the glass part of the door. He was striding down the road, his head high.

I sat down, looked out. Trees, dandelions, daisies. A year ago Sini and I had been here, on this road, on our way back to Winterswijk. Not a bad year, the first one. Just a little difficult. I had said good-bye to so many people—the Oostervelds, Sini, Rachel.

There was Mother now. She cared about me. Just couldn't admit it—wasn't that kind of person. Maybe later she would come straight out and tell me, when she had known me longer. Then I'd be sure. "You're not going back to Usselo for a long time," she'd say the minute I came in. "I want you home."

I'd ask her about the summer. I had promised Johan I would. I didn't want to spend all my vacations in Usselo though. Gloomily I stared out the window. What about Walcheren? The first reeds would be up already. And the dikes were sturdy again. I could climb on one, all the way to the top, and look and look. Water, sailboats, sea gulls, sky. . . But I could see land, too. Hawthorn hedges, gardens, pinks, yellows. And the people, all back, wearing their costumes—pretty ones, long skirts, colorful blouses, lace caps. I could even hear some of the men and women practicing. The annual band concert was coming up. Listen . . . music: a clarinet, a trombone—new instruments, replacing those that had been washed into the North Sea. Walcheren. Had wanted to go there for so long. I could even go by myself, couldn't I . . . when I was old enough. Only fourteen next month.

And on the bus went, while in the ruins of Nuremberg, Hitler's closest friends and helpers were still on trial. So many crimes, horrible ones. Deaths. Millions. In so many ways. And places. But other crimes as well, not only deaths, ones you couldn't even see.

In Winterswijk the baker would be on his way to Mrs. Menko's with a fresh loaf of bread. She'd give away the rest of yesterday's, which she would hardly have touched, but not until he had rung her bell, and she was sure she had a new loaf. "I know it's crazy, but it makes me feel safe." She still couldn't talk about what had happened to her. Only cry. "Does everyone have to go through it personally before people will stop wars? Please, please."

On, past woods where signs warned people to stay out—land mines. And on, while in Amsterdam the barrel organ went from street to street, a dog next to it carrying a cup. Coins plopping in. "Thank you." And the man kept on turning the wheel, quicker, releasing more ting-tingly music. "Thank you, thank you." On, and on, on, while another railroad bridge somewhere in Holland had just been repaired, and across it, *ke-chunk, ke-chunk*, went another train, decorated, and crowded with officials wearing suits that were no longer worn-out and patched. Those old suits were on scarecrows now, out in the fields. There, the bus just passed one. Cap, jacket—looking like a farmer from a distance.

Through a mist of tears, more things flashed by. Had trouble seeing them. Johan. What was he doing now? Home? No, plowing probably. The potatoes. . . . Just as he had all the other springs since he was eleven.

"I began work early in life, Annie, not like most other kids. I did play soccer though, a couple of times. You should've seen me. I could've become a real good player. Damned if it isn't true. If I could have played more often. But that's the way it was, with Pa sick all the time. Did I ever tell you I did very well in school? Could have become a teacher —that's how well. But Annie, you know what I really wanted to be? A vet. I've got a special feeling for animals, I guess you can say."

Furrows now, in his field. The soil soft, crumbly. "C'mon, horse, come. We've got to move on."

Me, too. Move on, go places, see things. Maybe Johan was thinking about something pleasant now, too. The secret, Johan, the tractor. Please, Johan, think about that. Please.

I couldn't see anything now, too many tears. Later, I'd tell him about it; where I had been, what I had seen. "That island, Johan, Walcheren. I stood on top of the dike . . . looked . . . miles of water straight ahead of me. Far away, it was darker. Could be land. A boat. Anything. . . ." Later, Johan, later.

ABOUT THE AUTHOR

Johanna Reiss was born and brought up in Holland. After she was graduated from college, she taught elementary school for several years before coming to the United States to live. Her first book for children, *The Upstairs Room*, was a Newbery Honor Book, an American Library Association Notable Children's Book, and a Jane Addams Peace Association Honor Book, and it won the Jewish Book Council Juvenile Book Award and the Buxtehuder Bulle, a prestigious German children's book award.

Mrs. Reiss writes that soon after she had finished *The Upstairs Room*, she found "there was still something I wanted to say, something that was as meaningful to me as the story I had told in the first book, the story of a war. 'The fighting has stopped'; 'Peace treaty signed,' newspapers announce at the conclusion of every war. From a political point of view, the war is over, but in another sense it has not really ended. People are fragile. They are strong, too, but wars leave emotional scars that take a long time to heal, generations perhaps. I know this to be true of myself, and of others. And out of those feelings came *The Journey Back*, a story of the aftermath of the Second World War."

Though Mrs. Reiss lives with her daughters in New York City, they make frequent visits to Holland to visit Mrs. Reiss's sisters, Rachel and Sini, and Johan and Dientje Oosterveld.